WIND

MILLS & BOON LIMITED
ETON HOUSE 18–24 PARADISE ROAD
RICHMOND SURREY TW9 1SR

All the characters in this book have no existence outside the imagination of the Author, and have no relation whatsoever to anyone bearing the same name or names. They are not even distantly inspired by any individual known or unknown to the Author, and all the incidents are pure invention.

All Rights Reserved. The text of this publication or any part thereof may not be reproduced or transmitted in any form or by any means, electronic or mechanical, including photocopying, recording, storage in an information retrieval system, or otherwise, without the written permission of the publisher.

This book is sold subject to the condition that it shall not, by way of trade or otherwise, be lent, resold, hired out or otherwise circulated without the prior consent of the publisher in any form of binding or cover other than that in which it is published and without a similar condition including this condition being imposed on the subsequent purchaser.

First published in Great Britain 1992 by Mills & Boon Limited

© Clare Lavenham 1992

Australian copyright 1992 Philippine copyright 1992 This edition 1992

ISBN 0 263 77591 7

Set in 10½ on 12½ pt Linotron Palatino 03-9203-44178 Typeset in Great Britain by Centracet, Cambridge Made and printed in Great Britain

CHAPTER ONE

THE telephone call from Gibraltar came, most inconveniently, when Tracy was alone in the house and in the middle of washing her hair. At first she was tempted to ignore it, but it occurred her that it might be from the nursing agency with the offer of a new job.

She had been at home now for two weeks and was beginning to feel like work again, though she had enjoyed the rest after three strenuous cases in a row. The family home was comfortable, but it was also lonely, since both her parents had full-time jobs. It was six years since she had left Eastbridge to start her training at a big London hospital, and she had inevitably lost touch with many of her old friends.

Hastily bundling her dripping hair into a huge terry towelling turban, Tracy ran downstairs and snatched up the reciever.

The call was not from the agency. Her breathless 'hello' was answered by a voice she recognised and at the same time disbelieved, a voice which sent the wheels of memory turning back over the years to the wedding of Nerina, her best friend at the hospital, to Captain Charles Maxwell. Tracy had been a bridesmaid, and had lost her heart—very briefly—to the handsome fair-haired officer.

'I'm sorry to trouble you,' said the voice, 'but I'm very anxious to get in touch with Tracy Arnold. I wondered if you could help.'

'This is Tracy speaking.'

There was an astonished pause and then Charles exclaimed, 'Good lord—what a piece of luck!' He hurriedly gave his name. 'Does your being at home mean you're free just now?'

'I expect to be starting a new job any minute. I was just waiting——'

'You're booked, then?'

He had sounded extraordinarily disappointed, and Tracy quickly put him right. 'Why do you want to know?' she went on. '*You* surely haven't got a job for me?'

'As a matter of fact, I have.' His distress reached her clearly across the great land mass of Europe. 'It's Nerina——'

'She's ill?'

'Not exactly ill, but she's very far from OK, I'm afraid. She had a fall when she was out birdwatching down at Europa Point and did something to her back. She's got to lie flat for goodness knows how long.'

'I didn't know she was interested in birds,' said Tracy.

'It's only since we came to Gib. I think she felt she needed a new pastime. We've got a nanny for Jamie, you see, so she doesn't have a lot to do.'

Tracy was momentarily sidetracked as she thought of the adorable two-year-old who was her godson. At least, he looked adorable in photographs, but she hadn't seen him since his christening. Hastily switching her attention back to the business in hand, she expressed her concern at Charles's news.

'Poor Nerina, she'll hate being inactive. Is she at home, then, that you want me to come and look after her?'

'She's in hospital at the moment and absolutely hating it. The surgeon would let her come home if there was a trained nurse to take charge.' His voice changed and became pleading. 'You *will* come, Tracy love, won't you? There's no one she'd rather have.'

'Of course I'll come! I'll tell the agency not to send me any jobs for the present and catch the first plane to Gibraltar. Give Nerina my love, Charles.'

'Can I keep a little for myself?' he asked, apparently so cheered by her acceptance that he was able to revert to a more normal manner.

Tracy was not deceived. He had been genuinely upset and worried when he came on the line, but he had an optimistic temperament which helped him to look on the bright side. The flirtatious reply merely meant he was feeling much better. At least, she hoped so.

A trickle of water had escaped from the turban and was creeping down her neck. She said goodbye quickly and went thoughtfully back upstairs, her mind busy with memories of the past.

She and Nerina had been in the same set all

through their hospital training and their friendship had never faltered, but they had inevitably seen little of each other after Nerina married into the Army. Tracy had stayed with them once in Germany and had been relieved to find she had got over her crush on Charles, though she still found him dangerously attractive. Now that she was going to see so much more of him she hoped devoutly she would be able to remain detached.

She had just finished blow-drying her beech-brown hair when she heard the front door shut with a sharp snick and knew her mother had returned from the High School where she was head of English.

'Hi!' Tracy appeared at the top of the stairs and looked down into the hall where Joan Arnold was taking off the smart navy jacket she had worn as a protection against the cold early spring wind.

A faded blonde, Joan's only good feature was the wide grey eyes which her daughter had inherited. She looked up and acknowledged the greeting, adding a question.

'Heard anything from the agency?'

'No, but I've got a job.' Tracy descended to the hall and burst into an account of her phone call. 'I don't like the sound of it at all, Mum. Backs are so easily upset and often take ages to put right.'

'It'll give you something to do, anyway. I could tell you were getting restless.'

Not a word of sympathy for Nerina, Tracy thought bitterly, yet if there had been a serious accident at her school her mother would have been full of it.

She said tersely, 'I'd better ring up Gatwick and book a seat on a plane leaving as early as possible tomorrow—if you think you can put up with me until then.'

'Now you're just being silly.' Joan sighed, and went into the kitchen to begin preparations for the evening meal.

Tracy noticed the sigh and regretted her impulsive remark. Her mother didn't have an easy life. The school was very demanding, and she always arrived home tired, and reluctant to cope with domestic matters. Her husband had a much easier time of it, with a good job in insurance, but he never offered to help. It was hardly surprising that they didn't get on and now led almost completely separate lives.

Sometimes Tracy marvelled that they had stayed together under the same roof after their three children became independent of them. She could only suppose it was habit, and because neither of them wanted to marry anyone else. When she was at home between jobs it worried her quite a lot, and she longed for a happy home background with her parents still sharing the marital bed.

Looking round, though, she had to admit that that sort of situation wasn't exactly thick on the ground. Her sister had divorced after only eighteen months of marriage, and her brother lived with a succession of girlfriends, all of them free as air. She had decided long ago that it was much better to keep a tight grip on her heart and concentrate on her career.

In view of that eminently sensible and hard-headed decision, it was surprising that she appeared to be vulnerable enough to fall for anyone like Charles Maxwell! Next time anything like that happened—and she had an uneasy feeling that it might—she hoped the man wouldn't be married. Then maybe they could enjoy a light-hearted affair and hurt no one.

It didn't occur to her that they might hurt themselves.

Laying the table in the dining annexe, she found her thoughts returning to Nerina's accident. Would there be a downstairs room in Charles's house which could be turned into a temporary bedroom? Would the hospital be willing to lend a bed and equipment? She didn't even know if Nerina was in a military hospital or a civilian one, but if it was the former no doubt things would be easier to arrange for the wife of an officer.

By this time tomorrow she would be in Gilbraltar and all her questions would be answered.

Gatwick was the usual bedlam, and all the luggage trolleys seemed to be in use. Not knowing how long she would be away, Tracy had packed a good-sized suitcase, and she also had bulging hand luggage. As she queued to have the case checked in, she hoped fervently that she wouldn't have to pay excess. Agency nursing was well paid, but when you were on holiday you got no pay at all, and she had recently indulged in an orgy of shopping for summer clothes. They would come in handy in the Mediterranean climate of Gibraltar, and she could not regret her extravagance.

The man at the head of the queue was having an argument with the girl at the desk and everyone had to wait. Resigned, Tracy put her case down and glanced idly round.

Her attention was immediately caught by a middle-aged woman who, with ashen face, was being supported by the man with her. He was looking round anxiously for an unoccupied seat, but before he could locate one a much younger man appeared on her other side and instantly took charge of the situation.

He was very tall, dark-haired and dressed in expensive-looking casual clothes. In no time at all he had cleared a space on the nearest bench and was steering the half-fainting woman towards it. Tracy watched with professional interest as he laid his fingers on the limp wrist and began to check the pulse.

A doctor? His air of authority seemed to suggest it. She continued to study the scene as he questioned the man, who was fumbling in his pocket. Just as he produced a small phial, the queue moved on and Tracy lost sight of the little group. By the time she had boarded the plane and—miraculously—obtained a window seat, she had almost forgotten it.

She was struggling to stow her hand luggage down by her feet when a voice spoke beside her.

'There really isn't room down there. Do let me put it on the rack for you.'

It was the tall dark man, obviously intending to take the seat next to her, and Tracy, who liked to make her own arrangements, reacted instinctively against the slight hint of bossiness.

'Thank you, but I don't want it on the rack. It's got my book in it and—and other things I might need.'

'It's a three-hour flight to Gibraltar,' he pointed out, 'and you won't be able to stretch your legs.'

'I shall be OK,' she insisted.

He raised his eyebrows, which were dark like his hair and slanted in an interesting way towards a well-shaped nose. 'You prefer to be uncomfortable?'

There had been a ripple of amusement in his voice and Tracy felt herself flushing. To answer, 'Yes, I do!' would be ridiculous, though she was greatly tempted to do so. Instead she merely shrugged and turned towards the window. To her relief he unfolded his newspaper and gave it his full attention.

It was an hour before they spoke again.

During that time Tracy had managed, with a great deal of difficulty, to extract her book and appear to bury herself in it. The fact that her absorption *was* only apparent annoyed her. At first she couldn't stop thinking about Nerina, which was pointless when she would soon know all the details, and then she became increasingly aware of the man at her side.

Every time he turned the pages of his paper, or brushed against her arm, or shifted his feet— gloriously unimpeded by luggage since his briefcase rested correctly on the rack—her attention was caught in the most maddening way.

Usually in planes and trains she liked to talk to someone, and to sit so close to a fellow passenger in total silence she found disturbing. Consequently she waited until he had apparently finished reading and then directed a question at him.

'What happened to the lady at Gatwick who was feeling unwell?'

He turned to her in surprise. 'How do you know about that?'

'I was watching from the luggage queue, but we moved on before the end of it,' Tracy explained.

'Well, you didn't miss any drama. She has angina—recently diagnosed—and her husband was given medication to administer if she had an attack of that sort. Because it hadn't happened like that before, the poor chap got in a fluster and forgot all about his instructions. It was a good thing I was on the spot, or she might have found herself whisked off to hospital.'

Tracy felt impelled to fly to the husband's defence. 'Angina can be very frightening, and he was apparently inexperienced in dealing with it. I should think he'll remember all right next time.'

'I sincerely hope so, for his wife's sake,' he said quietly. He paused and she could feel his eyes studying her, but she kept her own gaze on the window. 'Do *you* have any experience of angina?' he asked.

'Oh, yes—quite a lot,' Tracy assured him airily.

She was about to add, 'I'm a nurse,' but she caught the words back. More than ever convinced he was a doctor, she had no desire to embark on a medical conversation with him. It would inevitably involve explaining why she was going to Gibraltar, and she didn't want to talk about Nerina until she had more information. Besides, he might turn out to be one of those doctors who considered nurses existed on a lower plane than themselves. Nowadays it was mostly ageing consultants who felt like that, but Tracy had come across a few younger men who shared their views.

Ignoring the fact that she had no grounds for thinking her neighbour was one of them, she reopened her book and kept her attention firmly fixed on it until the plane began slowly descending over Gibraltar.

It was impossible not to feel thrilled by her first sight of the famous Rock. No doubt it would look even more dramatic from the sea, but she was quite prepared to make do with her present view of the angular slab which reared up from a narrow coastal plain and appeared totally impregnable on all sides.

The man beside her leaned across and looked down.

'Extraordinary airport,' he commented. 'So important and so busy, yet with a public road right across the runway. Just like a railway level crossing on a bigger scale.'

Tracy turned in astonishment. 'That's absolutely amazing! I can't imagine anything more inconvenient. What on earth do they do when a plane wants to land?'

'Close the road of course.'

Feeling she had asked a silly question, she returned her attention to the window. The weather appeared to be superb, cloudless blue sky and blue sea to match, and when they landed and the door was opened a wave of balmy air wafted in, making it seem that summer had suddenly arrived.

The doctor—if that was what he was—went off without a word, encumbered only by his briefcase. Struggling with coat, handbag and the overloaded holdall, Tracy did not blame him for not offering to help. She hadn't been exactly encouraging when he wanted to put her hand luggage on the rack! She glimpsed him again in the Customs shed, where he appeared to have no suitcase to interest the officials, and after that he vanished from the scene, at the same time going completely out of her mind.

Charles, a blond giant of a man, was waiting for her, and she went forward eagerly to greet him.

'It's great to see you, Tracy.' He bent his head and gave her a resounding kiss. 'Welcome to Gib! I only wish you were here for a different reason.'

She returned the salutation with pleasure, glad to find her emotions completely unstirred, and handed over her luggage. They walked towards the car park chatting like the old friends that they were, and it was not until they were driving away from the airport that Tracy asked the question which was in the forefront of her mind.

'How's Nerina?'

'Just the same. The orthopaedist warned us it would be a long business and we must be patient, but I'd feel much happier if there was some sign of improvement. Seeing her lying there, looking so frail——' Charles broke off and cleared his throat. 'Perhaps she'll perk up now you've come, Tracy.'

'I'll certainly do my best, and I expect being allowed home will help.' She paused as he negotiated a tangle of traffic in the narrow road, then continued, 'It's terribly frustrating just to be told to rest, but where somebody's back is concerned it's much better than having an operation. Surgeons are never very keen on interfering with the spine.'

'The chap we've got never even mentioned it. All he said was that we've got to be patient.'

Charles was a splendid Army officer, Tracy knew, but his medical knowledge was nil. She made no attempt to go into details and instead asked when she could see Nerina.

'Just as soon as you like. I would suggest some lunch first and then I'll drive you to the hospital.'

Conversation lapsed as Tracey gave her attention to her surroundings. They appeared to be driving up the Rock, but as there were houses scattered everywhere she assumed it would not be too hair-raising. Down below she could see the long straight road which crossed the airport and, on the other side of it, went on to Spain. The runway, she now noticed, appeared to be built out into the sea. She was glad she had not realised that at the time.

'Here we are!' Charles halted before a pleasant house coloured pinkish-cream. 'How long is it since you saw Jamie?'

'Not since he was angelic in a christening robe.'

'He's far from angelic now, but Donna seems to manage him all right.' He got out and began to get her luggage out of the boot.

'Daddy!' A little boy with Nerina's dark wavy hair and big brown eyes came running round the side of the house. He flung his arms round his father's legs and clung tightly, laughing with pleasure.

A girl with gingerish hair hanging loose came hurrying into view and disentangled the tiny hands, which were gripping out of all proportion to their size.

'How can Daddy walk when you hang on to him like that?' She picked the child up, ignoring his protests. 'He'll talk to you later, but at present you must let him unload the car.'

Tracy looked at her with interest and encountered the frank stare of greenish-hazel eyes as Donna stood just inside the gate with Jamie in her arms. She was very young and pretty in rather an ordinary sort of way, with a round face and pert nose. Tracy hoped they would get on. In her experience nannies could sometimes be difficult.

'Hello!' She smiled and lightly touched the little boy's dark head, whereupon he promptly buried his face in the girl's shoulder.

'He's shy,' she said unnecessarily. 'But he's a very friendly child usually, so I expect he'll soon get to know you.'

Had she sounded just the least little bit patronising? Deciding it was her imagination, Tracy said casually, 'He's my godson, actually, so I'd like to be friends with him.' She hesitated, then added, 'I expect he misses his mummy.'

'He's got me,' Donna pointed out sharply. 'At this stage children need continuity in their lives, and a nanny can often provide that better than a mother.'

It was often the case, Tracy knew, but she didn't like to hear it applied to this family. Nerina, she was sure, was an adoring mother and must be hating the separation from her child.

'I expect you take Jamie to see her,' she suggested.

'Oh, yes, and I've explained it all to him very

carefully, so I don't think Nerina's accident will have any lasting effect on him.' Donna turned and led the way towards the wide open front door. 'I see Charles has finished unloading your luggage, so I'll take you up to your room. You'll want to freshen up before lunch.'

As she followed behind the slim figure in a short yellow dress—no uniform for Donna, apparently—Tracy was half amused, half irritated by the girl's cool assumption of the role of hostess. It was, after all, completely natural for her to show the newcomer to her room when the real hostess was flat on her back in hospital.

It was the way she did it that Tracy didn't like.

The Military Hospital was a beautiful building, perfectly proportioned and very well looked after. In the garden bougainvillaea blazed against the grey-green of eucalyptus, and cacti stood stiffly in the beds waiting for summer. Inside, it was light and airy with pot plants everywhere in the corridors. Walking beside Charles, Tracy glimpsed small modern wards and nurses in white dresses, but as the wife of an officer Nerina had a private room.

For a moment she stood poised in the doorway, grappling with an unexpected wave of emotion. This was a Nerina she had difficulty in recognising. The dark curls had been shaved on one side of her head and a line of stitches was visible. There were yellowish patches on the forehead caused by fading bruises, and signs of a once vivid black eye. Otherwise Nerina's face was unmarked, but so pale that even the lovely passionate mouth seemed bloodless. She lay quite flat, her slight body scarcely lifting the bedclothes on the high hospital bed.

'Oh, Tracy, I'm so glad to see you!' A thin hand was extended and the visitor went forward quickly to grasp it.

'I can't exactly say I'm glad to be here,' Tracy forced a smile, 'but you know what I mean. I should have been really upset if I'd had to tell Charles I was in the middle of a case and couldn't come.'

'Me too.' Nerina wrinkled her nose in a rueful grimace. 'They've been terribly kind to me here, but I just can't wait to get back to my own home. I don't like being regulated and having things done by the clock, and I miss Jamie most dreadfully. At home I shall be able to see him whenever I want.'

Tracy murmured a suitable reply and hoped the little boy could be made to understand that he mustn't climb about on his mummy's bed the way he was probably used to. As she sat down in the bedside chair, Charles came forward to kiss his wife.

'I'm sure you and Tracy will have a lot to talk about, and I shall feel thoroughly in the way——'

'Bored, you mean!' Nerina interrupted with a smile.

He brushed the comment aside. 'So I'm going to leave you two on your own while I see to a few things at the barracks. I'll be back in about an hour. OK, darling?'

As he turned to go, Tracy suddenly remembered that nothing had been said about her very necessary interview with the orthopaedist. It was important that she should be put thoroughly in the picture, and she hoped an appointment had been made.

Charles looked vague when she questioned him. 'You'll have to ask the sister about that, but I don't reckon he's likely to be here in the afternoon. For one thing, he's attached to the civilian hospital, not this one, and for another he's probably seeing patients at those posh consulting-rooms he's got at the top of Main Street.' Poised in the doorway, he waved a nonchalant hand. 'See you!'

'Poor Charles,' said Nerina when he had vanished. 'This has been a terrible time for him.'

'Worse for you!'

'Well, yes, but he does so hate people not being fit and well. He's so healthy himself that he doesn't feel at home with invalids, and it can't be much fun not being able to get into bed with his wife, let alone make love to her.' Nerina's voice quivered.

'I expect you miss it too,' Tracy said gently

'I'm just beginning to. At first I couldn't care less about sex. All I worried about was getting from one day to the next, but it's different now that I feel better in myself, as they say.' Her brown eyes filled with tears and she brushed them away impatiently.

Tracy squeezed her hand and changed the subject. 'I haven't had time to find out what arrangements Charles has made for your coming home. Is there a downstairs room which can be made into a bedroom?'

'Only the little dining-room where I expect you had your lunch. I can't take over the drawing-room and turn everybody else out.'

Tracy thought back and tried to visualise the small room without a dining-table. It still seemed very cramped, and with a bed in it she had an idea it would be nearly impossible. She would have to make it work, though. She'd got to, for Nerina's sake.

'It overlooks the garden, anyway,' she said cheerfully. 'That will be nice.'

'I expect you think that's pretty small too, but you won't realise how lucky we are to have one. Most people haven't got room. Every little flat space on the Rock—except really high up, of course—has a house on it. You'll see it all when Charles finds time to show you round.' Nerina changed the subject abruptly. 'What did you think of Jamie? Isn't he gorgeous?' Without waiting for an answer, she went rushing on, 'Oh Tracy, I can't tell you how I'm longing to be able to do things for him again! Play with him, and put him to bed—and even take him to the toilet.'

Tracy hesitated, then pointed out carefully, 'I don't suppose you did a lot of that sort of thing even before the accident. I expect Donna took charge most of the time, didn't she? She seems a very capable girl.'

Was it her imagination, or did a faint shadow cross Nerina's face? Whatever her thoughts, she only said briefly, 'Oh, yes, I'm lucky to have her.'

Tracy did not pursue the matter of Donna's capabilities. Instead, she asked curiously, 'What's this great man like who's going to tell me all I need to know about the state of your back? Do you like him?'

'I do now, but at first, while I was still concussed, he was just one of the faces that swam about above my bed. It was a day or two before I felt able to sort them out, and naturally I started with the nurses. Then I discovered that the boss was a man called Andrew Lincoln. Giving him a name has made him seem a bit more human, but I still feel like a goldfish in a bowl when they all stand round my bed and stare at me.'

'They say it's good for medical people to have a turn at being patients,' Tracy reminded her with a smile.

'Since I gave up nursing three years ago, I don't see it applies to me.' Nerina smiled, and suddenly they plunged into an orgy of reminiscing about their hospital days.

They were still at it when it occurred to Tracy that she ought to find out from the nursing staff if she could see Mr Lincoln tomorrow. Excusing herself a little while before Charles was due back, she went in search of someone in authority who might be able to tell her.

Wandering down a side corridor, she came to an open door of what must surely be Sister's office. A dark-haired nurse was at the desk, and she looked up enquiringly.

'Can I help you?'

Relieved to be addressed in perfect English, Tracy explained her problem.

'It's all arranged for you.' The nurse consulted a desk diary. 'Tomorrow morning at ten o'clock. Mr Lincoln will see you before he does his round, so if you report here a few minutes before that time you can wait in this office. It is OK?'

'Perfectly OK, thank you.' Tracy smiled and went in search of Charles.

'You'll have to take a taxi,' he told her. 'I shall be busy in the morning, but Donna will order one for you if you ask her.'

'Can't I do it myself?'

'Why, yes, of course, if you wish.' He sounded surprised. 'You'll find that English is spoken a great deal in Gib both by the Spanish and Gibraltarians, and a lot of the inhabitants *are* English, so you'll have no problem.'

Tracy had no difficulty at all in ordering her taxi. But the problem she had to face when she met Mr Lincoln was a different matter.

CHAPTER TWO

THE taxi was late, and Tracy watched from the window in a fever of impatience. It would be a terribly bad start not to be punctual for her interview.

'You should have allowed a ten-minute margin,' Donna informed her. 'The taxi-drivers are very obliging but a bit hazy about time. They're mostly Spanish, you see.'

'Now she tells me!' Tracy didn't try to hide her exasperation.

'I'd have made the phone call if you'd asked me.' Donna tossed back her shining curtain of hair and gently removed a ball of knitting wool from Jamie's reluctant hands.

Fortunately the car arrived at that moment and Tracy went hurrying out. It was, as she already knew, a short drive to the hospital and they were there within a few minutes, which was hardly long enough for her to collect her thoughts and present an appearance of coolness and calm.

In the corridor she met an obviously English fair-haired sister whose eyes flickered doubtfully over Tracy's green-and-white striped dress. She had been undecided whether to wear uniform but to do so when she was not on duty seemed unnecessary.

After all, her ability to look after Nerina in a professional manner didn't depend on her clothes.

'Nurse Arnold?' the sister said dubiously.

Tracy admitted her identity, adding breathlessly, 'I'm sorry I'm late, but the taxi——'

'Mr Lincoln is in the office, whiling away the time by going through some notes.' Unexpectedly, Sister smiled. 'Don't look so alarmed! He's not the sort to hold it against you.'

Did her feelings show as plainly as that? Tracy got a grip on herself and followed her guide until she once more arrived at the open door of the office she remembered from yesterday.

'Nurse Arnold is here, sir.'

Sister was a well-built young woman and, as she stood in the doorway, completely hid the man at the desk from Tracy's view. But there was something horribly familiar about the voice that replied.

'And about time too!'

The next moment Tracy was staring in horror at the dark man she had sat next to on the plane.

She had, she remembered, guessed he was a doctor, but her imagination had done nothing to prepare her for the shock of discovering he was the orthopaedic surgeon in charge of Nerina, the man she would have to work under and do her best to please.

With a mental shrug, she pulled herself together. He had given no sign of recognising her, and as far as she knew he had never even glanced at her face. Besides, she had been wearing a T-shirt and jeans then, with her light brown hair loose on her shoulders; now it was fastened back with a band, and she looked, she hoped, impeccably neat and tidy. At least she would be able to make a fresh start.

It was a pity about the lack of uniform, though. It would have boosted her morale.

'I'll be with you in a moment, Nurse,' Mr Lincoln said, shuffling his papers.

Tracy sat down without being invited and automatically folded her hands in her lap as she had done when she was a student nurse being talked at by a high-up nursing officer. With some difficulty, she avoided staring at him and instead allowed her eyes to wander round the room, which did not prove very rewarding, since it was exactly like all the sisters' offices she had known in the past.

'Well now,' he said abruptly, almost making her jump. He leaned back in the chair, resting his elbows on the arms and looking at her over tented fingers. 'I've got something important I want to discuss with you.'

Tracy looked at him silently, wondering what on earth he meant, and met the disconcerting stare of Irish blue eyes under long curling lashes. Their expression was extremely serious, and she felt a twinge of fear. Was there something wrong with Nerina she didn't know about?

Apparently he sensed her reaction, for he smiled briefly and said, 'Don't look so alarmed! I'm not talking about your friend's physical condition. As far as that's concerned she would definitely be better kept in hospital for a little longer.'

'I don't understand. I was under the impression you thought it was a good idea for her to go home.' Tracy tilted her chin and looked across the desk at him with an air of challenge.

'Very likely her husband gave you that impression. I've certainly done my best to let him think I was in favour of the move.' Andrew Lincoln hesitated, then went on reluctantly, 'I didn't want him to get a hint of my—suspicions, in case they turned out to be unfounded.'

'Suspicions!' Tracy was aghast, her thoughts leaping wildly in all directions. 'Why did you give your permission for Nerina to be discharged if you were—uneasy about it?'

The surgeon leaned forward, scattering his pile of papers. 'I had to choose between Nerina's physical needs, which—as I've already mentioned— would be better served in hospital, and her mental state——'

'*Mental?*' Tracy gasped.

'Don't look so shocked,' he apologised quickly. 'I meant nothing sinister—only that she seems very worried about something, and for some reason— which may be clearer to you than it is to me—she has an abnormally strong desire to return home.'

'I expect she misses her little boy.'

'Yes, indeed she must, but I think it's more than that.' He paused, fixing Tracy with a penetrating blue gaze which she found disconcerting. 'I believe you're a close friend of the family. Perhaps you can enlighten me.'

She shook her head helplessly, and Andrew Lincoln gave her a clue as to the direction his thoughts were taking.

'Are her marital relations good?' he asked.

'Oh, *yes*!' The suggestion that they might not be startled her. 'At least, I've always believed them to be, but I haven't seen much of Nerina since she married.'

'She's got something on her mind, that's for sure, and I subscribe to the modern view that it's important to treat the whole of a patient and not merely the body. Unfortunately a surgeon has less opporunity to do that than a doctor.'

Tracy sat silent, turning it over in her mind and finding it more and more impossible to believe there was anything wrong with her friend's marriage. No doubt Mr Lincoln fancied himself as a psychiatrist, but he was making a mistake now, she was convinced.

Nerina had always been a home-loving girl, her sights set on marriage rather than a career in nursing. She just *hated* being in hospital, that was all. Tracy had come across people like that quite often, but a surgeon in a big hospital in the UK wouldn't have a clue about his patients' secret thoughts. Only the nurses had that kind of knowledge.

In a small place like this it would be different.

Very likely the orthopaedist didn't have enough to do.

'I can see you think I've been talking a load of rubbish,' Andrew Lincoln said unexpectedly.

Tracy started and flushed. To her surprise she actually discovered a twinkle in his eyes and she had a sudden impulse towards honesty.

'I'm afraid I do think that, Mr Lincoln, though I wouldn't have put it quite so frankly. You haven't convinced me that Nerina has anything more than a rather strong desire to go home.'

The twinkle became more pronounced. 'That obstinacy of yours will land you in real trouble one of these days,' he observed blandly.

'What do you mean?' she gasped and, to her annoyance, began to stammer with embarrassment. 'I—I didn't think——'

'That I'd recognised you? I didn't at first, but gradually it began to dawn on me that we'd met on the plane. You were stubborn about letting me stow your holdall for you, and you're being equally stubborn about your friend's mental state.' Suddenly he was serious again. 'I only hope that this time you're right, that's all.'

Tracy opened her mouth to say firmly, 'Of course I am', and found herself changing it into, 'I hope so too.'

What was the matter with her? Surely she wasn't going to let this amateur psychiatrist instil his own doubts into her? There was nothing wrong with the Maxwells' marriage! Absolutely nothing.

Nerina was homesick and longing to see more of Jamie. It was as simple as that.

'When do you think the move can be made?' she asked.

'As soon as everything is ready to receive the patient. The hospital is willing to lend a bed and traction equipment, and a physiotherapist will attend regularly. The rest is up to you.'

'I'll do my best,' she promised, and found herself making an inner vow to look out for signs of tension between Nerina and Charles. She was almost certain she wouldn't find any, and it would be eminently satisfactory to prove Mr Lincoln wrong.

Nerina came home the following afternoon. In the meantime Tracy had worked hard organising the household, helped enthusiastically by Jamie— though there was little he could do—and with some reluctance, so she fancied, by Donna. The two porters from the hospital moved the dining-table into the drawing-room for them, and erected the bed and its equipment, arguing with each other in Spanish as they worked.

Donna stood surveying their handiwork and idly moved the door backwards and forwards. 'It's only just possible to open and shut it,' she observed.

'I know that!' Tracy tried not to snap. 'I'm only thankful it *is* just possible.'

'What are you going to put things on? Washing bowls and all that?'

'The sideboard, of course,' said Tracy. 'There's nothing else, but I shall have to find something to protect the polish.'

'I shouldn't bother if I were you. It's only Army furniture, so it doesn't matter.'

'It matters to me. I don't want to be held responsible for it having water stains all over it.' In a determinedly friendly tone, Tracy went on, 'If you've got nothing to do, would you mind helping me make the bed? I'm going to put Nerina's own sheets and duvet on it, so she'll feel she's really at home in spite of sleeping downstairs.'

Donna proved efficient at mitring corners and they worked together smoothly. When it was all done—pink sheets, frilly pillowcase on the single pillow, and toning floral duvet—both girls stood back to admire their handiwork.

'How long will Nerina have to sleep here?' Donna asked.

'Until she can manage the stairs.'

'You really think she'll get better? I mean, be able to walk and—and be a normal person again?'

'Oh, yes,' Tracy assured her confidently. 'It's only a matter of time, but don't ask me how long, because I don't know the answer. It could be weeks.'

There was no reply, but somehow it seemed to her that the nanny didn't appear displeased. And for the first time a dreadful suspicion flashed into her mind.

Had Charles exercised the same fatal attraction

for Donna as he had done for herself at the time of his marriage to Nerina? Because she was older and more mature, she had known how to cope with it, but for a girl probably still under twenty it would be different.

The more she thought about it, the more likely it seemed that Donna had been enjoying being alone in the house with Charles. Both the Spanish servants slept out, and Jamie didn't count.

Suddenly an even worse suggestion slid like a snake into her troubled thoughts. Donna was very attractive and Charles was a man of strong sexual appetite. He must have been finding his enforced celibacy trying.

Even so, surely he wouldn't console himself with Donna? It was unthinkable!

Ashamed that she *had* allowed herself to think of it, Tracy pushed the thought away with some violence, and blamed herself because her own jaundiced view of marriage had led her into wild imaginings. Just as wild as Mr Lincoln's notion that Nerina had marital problems. She might not even have thought of it if he hadn't already planted the idea in her mind. Tiresome man!

The sight of a huge bunch of brilliantly coloured flowers which Charles brought home at lunchtime helped her to put her suspicions aside, but she couldn't help studying him surreptitiously during the meal. He really did seem delighted that his wife was coming home.

'I'm taking the afternoon off,' he told the two

girls. 'Can't have Nerina returning without me to welcome her. You put the flowers in her room, didn't you, Tracy?' And when she confirmed it, he added fervently, 'I'm no end grateful to you for making this great occasion possible.'

'You'd have got another nurse instead of me if I hadn't been free,' she pointed out.

'It wouldn't have been the same, and Nerina certainly wouldn't have been so happy with a stranger. As it is, things have worked out really well, and now what we've got to do is concentrate on getting her up on her feet.'

Agreeing enthusiastically, Tracy stole a glance at Donna, but the nanny was busy supervising Jamie's joyful spooning up of ice cream and appeared to be paying no attention. Later, she sensibly suggested taking him out so that his mother could be installed before he saw her.

'We'll go to the paddling pool at Camp Bay—he loves that.' She glanced at Tracy. 'I've been using Nerina's Mini quite a lot while she's been in hospital.'

Tracy could think of nothing to say except, 'That's nice,' so she went off to put on a white uniform dress and her hospital belt. Nerina wouldn't like it, but she thought she ought to look official when the ambulance arrived.

After that there was nothing to do except wait.

Donna and Jamie did not return until teatime. By then an exhausted but radiant Nerina was settled in her makeshift bedroom. She was pleased with everything—the arrangements that had been made, the flowers, the presence of her husband in the welcoming party. Everything except Tracy's uniform.

'Why are you dressed up like that?' she wanted to know. 'I think of you as my friend, not a nurse.'

'It was only for the benefit of your escort,' Tracy explained. 'I'll go and change.'

Upstairs she slipped out of the offending garment and substituted a pair of white shorts and a blue sleeveless top which instantly turned her into a holidaymaker. Releasing her hair from its constricting band, she glanced in the mirror to check her make-up, then ran downstairs again.

'That's better!' Nerina smiled approval.

Glad that she had pleased her patient, Tracy settled down for a chat, completely unaware that later on she was going to regret her change of clothing.

It was half-past eight when Andrew Lincoln came to call. Dinner was over and Nerina was lightly dozing after the exciting day. The last thing her nurse expected was to find the consultant on the doorstep.

Tracy had opened the door merely because she happened to be nearest. Aghast, she stared at the tall figure very correctly dressed in a dark suit.

'Good evening er—Nurse.' His eyes briefly inspected the shorts. 'I called to see if Mrs Maxwell had suffered no ill effects from being moved.'

'Her temperature's slightly up.' Tracy held the door wider and ushered him in.

'That's only to be expected. If it hasn't settled down by this time tomorrow, let me know. I intend to keep in close touch.'

Tracy was puzzled. She would have expected the family doctor to take over now. Making no comment, she led him to the converted dining-room and showed him Nerina's chart which she had conscientiously made out.

He was very formal and correct, but when the visit was concluded and she was escorting him to his car, he suddenly unbent.

'Why were you so surprised to see me? After our conversation yesterday I would have expected you to take it for granted that I'd want to check up on my patient.' He halted with his hand on the gate.

'Consultants don't usually——'

'I'm not really a consultant, you know,' he said with a smile.

'Not?'

'No, though I'm hoping to become one as soon as possible after I'm back in England. Here I'm only a locum.'

'I see,' said Tracy.

'You don't see at all. How could you?' He glanced over her shoulder. 'Come and sit down on that garden seat for a moment and I'll explain.'

In a dream she followed him down a narrow path between flower beds, past a huge hibiscus bush already showing signs of buds, to where the seat gleamed white in the dusk.

'In London,' Mr Lincoln went on, 'I was an orthopaedic senior registrar, but I'm deputising for my uncle, who's normally in charge of the orthopaedic department at the civilian hospital here. Unfortunately he's got cardiac trouble and he asked me to hold the fort for him until he felt better and could return.' He sighed. 'I'm not at all sure he'll ever come back, but I have to go along with the fiction that he'll be a new man in a few weeks.'

'I see,' Tracy said again, and this time she saw a great deal more than she had actually been told. Whichever way you looked at it, Andrew Lincoln had interrupted his career to come to the rescue of a relative who might be nearing retirement age. It was extremely generous of him.

'Now that's cleared up,' he was saying briskly, 'I want to sort out another matter which is bothering me—your off-duty time. Do you realise you've let yourself in for both day and night duty? I'm sure it's against the rules of your nursing agency.'

'Oh yes,' Tracy agreed airily, 'but I wasn't sent here by the agency, so I can work twenty-four hours at a stretch if I like.'

'Even you wouldn't be that daft, surely?' he exclaimed.

She flung him an indignant look, but he was staring at her so intently that she looked away hastily.

'I don't suppose Nerina will need much attention

in the night, but for a few days at least I'm quite prepared for it. I shall snatch a nap in the afternoon when she's having hers—if necessary.'

'Stubborn again,' he muttered.

'When we've known each other a little longer, Mr Lincoln, you'll find that when I make up my mind I usually stick to it.'

Heavens, how appallingly pompous she'd sounded! Disgusted, Tracy went on in quite a different tone, 'It's not just that. I'm very fond of Nerina. We were very close before her marriage, and I want to do everything I can to help her regain her health and strength.'

He made no reply, but, to her surprise, she felt the light touch of his fingers on her hand. A strange sensation passed up her arm and she shivered.

Until then they had talked animatedly, flinging words back and forth at each other, but now an odd silence enveloped them. For the first time Tracy became aware of the beauty of the view. Although it was past sunset there was no real darkness anywhere. Not very far away the coast of Spain glowed with light, and there were other lights on the sea, moving red or green ones. Above their heads stars blazed in a clear sky, brighter than at home and looking larger too, and she remembered that Africa was only just across a narrow strait.

She jumped up suddenly. 'I must go in—Nerina might want me.'

'Hang on a minute—there's just one more thing.'

Andrew rose in a leisurely manner and restrained her by a hand on her shoulder. 'I have no intention of continuing to call you Nurse when you're wearing shorts—or any other form of non-uniform gear. Tracy is your name, I believe? In future I intend to use it, and I hope you'll stop calling me Mr Lincoln now you know I'm not really a consultant.'

'OK,' she said carelessly. 'I really must go in now. Goodnight—Andrew.'

During the next few days Tracy managed to establish a hospital routine without making it too obvious to the patient, the only difference being that she didn't serve meals at the abnormally early hours considered necessary by hospitals. Nerina was allowed to sleep until she woke naturally, and she had her lunch when the others were eating theirs, though Tracy stayed with her to make sure she didn't encounter difficulties. Liquids were the biggest problem, and she was obliged to use either a feeding cup or some other container with a bent straw.

Every morning after Charles had left for the barracks, Tracy unfastened the traction equipment and gave her patient a thorough but very gentle blanket bath, after which she sprinkled the slim body generously with talc and applied antiseptic cream to the pressure points.

'You're determined I shan't get bedsores,' Nerina said with a smile. 'I can't think why Andrew Lincoln thought I'd be better off in hospital.'

'I expect you'd have had a daily visit from one of the physios, even though you can't do much exercise at present,' said Tracy.

'He said he'd send a physiotherapist to visit me here as soon as I was strong enough, so I don't see I'm missing much. And just think what I'm gaining!'

Tracy looked thoughtfully at her friend and agreed that the move had done her good. Her eyes were brighter and there was a little colour in her cheeks, particularly in the evenings when Charles sat by her bed, holding her hand and chatting.

Maybe she really had been worrying about her husband left alone in the house with the nanny? If so, she must have been reassured by becoming once more part of the household.

She was a good patient, always apologising if she gave any extra trouble and never ringing her bell at night. Nevertheless Tracy got up at regular intervals to make sure she was not in need of attention and lying awake not wanting to be a nuisance.

Her own room was at the top of the stairs, and both doors were kept open. Once she heard Jamie cry out and met Donna on the landing, looking like a child herself in her short frilly nightdress. They did not speak, and Tracy went on downstairs. She found Nerina awake.

'I thought I heard Jamie,' she whispered. 'Is Donna seeing to him?'

'I met her on her way.' Tracy plumped up and

turned the single pillow which was all Nerina was allowed. 'From the sound of it I think he was probably dreaming.'

'She's such a good, conscientious girl. We're very lucky to have her to do everything for Jamie now I can't do one single damn thing.'

'You'll be able to before so very long, love.'

Tracy had spoken absently. She had been surprised at the fulsome praise. It *could* mean, of course, that Nerina felt she had been misjudging Donna in her mind and was unconsciously trying to make up for it. Tracy did not herself consider the nanny was anything special, except that she was undoubtedly devoted to her charge.

Thinking about it, she supposed she ought to tell Andrew about it when he called again, but she would have to be very guarded as he had never mentioned the nanny.

Nerina made it easy for her to have a private conversation with him by suggesting Tracy took him into the drawing-room and gave him coffee.

'You're doing a good job here, Tracy.' Andrew leaned back in a comfortable chair and looked her up and down appreciatively as she sat opposite him wearing a most unprofessional white sundress. 'Nerina seems much brighter, and I really believe it would be safe to conclude that whatever was worrying her has now gone.'

'I think so too.' She handed him a cup of black coffee and pushed the cream jug towards him. 'How about her physical condition?'

'That seems satisfactory too.' He paused, holding her gaze. 'In fact, I'm prepared to admit I was wrong in thinking she wouldn't get on so well at home.'

'That's very handsome of you!'

They both laughed, then Andrew changed the subject.

'You've been here nearly a week now and it's time you saw something of Gibraltar. I wouldn't mind betting you've been no farther than the garden so far.'

'I don't feel like taking the Mini out until I get some idea of the geography,' she protested.

'The local taxi-drivers do a great trade showing tourists all the sights, and they always start by indicating the exact spot in Casemates Square where the terrorists were shot.'

'Thanks very much—I'd absolutely love that!' said Tracy drily.

'Or, of course, I could offer you a personalised tour which I'm sure you'd find a great deal more interesting. Which would you prefer?'

He asked for it and she gave it to him. 'The taxi tour, of course,' she said promptly.

Once again they broke into laughter, and Tracy found herself agreeing to what he had called a personalised tour the following afternoon.

She couldn't help wondering how personal it would turn out to be.

CHAPTER THREE

TRACY wore a light pair of blue cotton trousers for her outing with Andrew, and carried a cardigan in case it was colder up on top. As she waited in the garden, listening for the sound of a car stopping, she wondered at the eagerness with which she was looking forward to the afternoon. It must, she decided, be because she was at last going to see something of the fascinating place where she had been living for the last week.

He arrived in a small but sporty-looking smoke-grey car with a sun-roof, ideal for the narrow streets and steep gradients of Gibraltar, and Tracy sank into the soft dark blue upholstery with a sigh of pleasure.

'It was clever of you to dress to match the car,' he commented.

'Feminine intuition, I expect.' She examined the dashboard with its array of gadgets. 'What an absolutely super car you've got!'

'The quickest way to a man's heart is to admire his——'

Tracy interrupted quickly, then wished she hadn't. 'That's not a route I'm planning on taking. My admiration was entirely spontaneous.'

'I never supposed anything else,' he assured her solemnly.

She was spared having to find an answer to that because an Army convoy suddenly came round the corner and Andrew had to draw in to the side of the road to let them get by.

'Is there anything you'd particularly like to see?' he asked when the line of nose-to-tail vehicles had passed.

'The monkeys,' Tracy said promptly.

'Apes,' he corrected.

'What?'

'They're Barbary apes, not monkeys—a zoological difference, I believe.' He turned his head and glanced at her. 'Do you really want to pay them a visit? It's a dreadfully touristy thing to do.'

'I don't care. I *am* a tourist, so why shouldn't I behave like one?'

'I can think of plenty of reasons, but never mind. We'll visit the apes after we've been to the top, but just remember they're apt to be vicious, so don't start stroking one and expect to hear an appreciative purr.'

Tracy would have liked to throw something at him, but instead she looked upwards through the open roof and caught a glimpse of the dramatic top of the Rock outlined against the usual bright blue sky.

'We surely can't drive all the way up?' she asked with a shade of apprehension in her voice.

'No, but there's a cable car, or, if you're feeling

energetic, we could climb the steps. It's much the most rewarding way of reaching the top. How about it?'

Her agreement was lost in a gasp of surprise as, without any warning, they plunged into the semi-darkness of a tunnel. After the dazzling sunshine outside, the electric light seemed very low-powered, but it was not long before they saw a patch of daylight in the distance.

'The whole Rock is riddled with these tunnels.' Andrew took up his role as guide. 'Not many public roads run through them, but the military use an enormous number as storerooms, arsenals, offices and even a small hospital. Some are newly excavated, but a lot go back to the time of the Napoleonic Wars.'

'It must be very useful to be able to provide more accommodation in that way instead of building it,' Tracy remarked.

'They certainly couldn't build. There's no room.'

'But what do they do with the material they've blasted out?'

'That's where it gets really cunning.' They swept into another tunnel. 'They dump all the surplus earth and rocks etc. on the edge of the sea and so create more land. No doubt that part of the runway which extends into the water was made that way.'

As they emerged into daylight again, he told her about the huge water catchment plants which caught rainwater and supplied all the taps in

Gibraltar. 'You see,' he explained, 'there are no rivers or springs, so every drop counts.'

'That's very interesting,' Tracy said politely.

'It's not—it's bloody boring! To you, I mean. Next time I start sounding off about the incredible use Gibraltar's made of its disadvantages, just tell me to get lost. Agreed?'

'No, it's not. I *ought* to learn about things like that or I'll have wasted my time here. I can't help it if I don't find them interesting, but I still need to know.'

Andrew let her have the last word and swung the car into a small car park.

'Is this where we start up the steps?' she asked, wrenching her eyes from the view and looking straight up the Rock instead. 'It looks a long way.'

'You haven't got any cardiac problems, have you?' he asked.

'Of course not!'

'Then just concentrate on how good it is for you to climb steps. All those people who take the lift even when they're only going to the first floor are just asking for trouble.'

She laughed and set off at a good speed which inevitably slackened quite soon. It was certainly a hard grind, but when they at last stepped on to the top she knew every bit of the effort had been worth it. Breathless and scarlet-faced, she wanted nothing more except just to stand and stare.

The whole world, so it seemed, lay around them. Spain was in shades of blue and green, its coastline white with hotels and houses, and North Africa offered the misty brown of the distant Atlas Mountains. All the rest was sea—the Atlantic Ocean moving restlessly and tipped with white, and the Mediterranean smooth dark blue.

'It's—it's breathtaking!' Tracy exclaimed, wishing she could think of a more original adjective.

'In more ways than one!' Andrew mopped his face. 'Let's sit down and recover.'

Except for the cable car terminus and a restaurant, the Rock was bare, but they found a patch of brownish, spiky grass and settled themselves on it. Andrew stretched out, looking relaxed and even sleepy, but Tracy sat rigidly upright, unwilling to take her eyes off that terrific view, oddly afraid to let herself copy his example.

She did not understand the reason, but she had never felt so unrelaxed in her life.

After a while she stopped staring around, and, noting that Andrew's eyes were closed, dared to study him instead. Even on the plane she had been aware of his physical magnetism, but now that his whole body was lying beside her, his bare forearm only an inch from her hand where it supported her weight, she found the experience more disturbing than she would have cared to admit.

Slowly, almost voluptuously, she allowed her gaze to drift over him. His face in repose was quite young, though there were tiny laughter lines at the corners of his eyes, and she judged him to be in his early thirties. His well-shaped nose was undoubtedly somewhat arrogant, but it was balanced by the gentle lines of his mouth. His shirt was open to the waist and showed a good thatch of dark hair, and Tracy's eyes hurriedly slid on towards his hands.

These were surgeons hands, not too large, the fingers not too long and very well manicured, the whole suggesting great capability. They looked like hands you could trust—but she had an uneasy feeling that, under certain circumstances, they might not be.

She was about to continue her investigation when a voice spoke suddenly and startled her so much she nearly jumped to her feet.

'Well? What's the verdict?'

Did the man have transparent eyelids? Or had he been watching her from beneath those ludicrously long lashes?

Blushing furiously, she pulled herself together and answered him equally lightly. 'The verdict is that you're far too good to be true. Good-looking, I mean, of course,' she added hastily.

'Thanks. You're not so bad yourself,' he said lazily. 'I like the neat shape of your nose and those clear grey eyes, but there's more than a hint of pigheadedness about the lines of the chin——'

'Shut up!' For the second time that afternoon Tracy longed to throw something at him. 'I think it's time we stopped analysing each other and started on the downward path——' She broke off in dismay. 'That is, I mean steps——' What on earth was the matter with her?

'Delighted!' Andrew put his arm round her and gave her a squeeze. 'It might be more fun if you'd really meant to say path, but the steps will do to be going on with. Lead the way, Tracy, and I'll follow.'

After that they descended in a silence which, far from being strained, was oddly companionable. They did not break it until they reached the car, when Tracy asked where they were going next.

'To see the apes, I think.' Andrew glanced at his watch. 'There isn't time to do justice to St Michael's Cave, so we'll keep that for another day. I imagine you don't want to be away from the house too long as it's the first time you've left Nerina?'

'Donna's promised to stay in this afternoon, but I said I'd be back at teatime,' she told him.

'So soon? I'd reckoned on giving you tea at one of the hotels, but that will also have to be kept for another day.'

He had been quite right when he described the apes as a tourist attraction, Tracy decided, as they parked again. There were stalls selling cards and souvenirs, and a photographer was urging people to have photographs taken with the animals. All she wanted was just to *see* them, since they were so famous. Hadn't they been on the Rock for hundreds of years?

Andrew confirmed it. 'I believe there's some idea that their continued existence here is connected with the British occupying Gib, but lots of places have that kind of tradition, so I don't suppose it means anything. Do you want to buy some food for them?'

'No, thanks. I doubt if they're underfed.'

They walked down a sloping path and came to a flat concreted area. Most of the apes seemed to have retired for an afternoon sleep, but one of them, medium-sized with longish brown fur and a surly expression, was squatting in the middle, busily shoving peanuts from a heap in front of him into his mouth, and ignoring the spectators.

'There doesn't seem to be anything to keep them in this one spot,' Tracy commented.

'There isn't. When they feel in the mood they roam all over the upper part of the Rock, stealing washing off the lines, and windscreen wipers, and people's necklaces. They're an absolute menace!'

'I'm glad Charles doesn't live as high up as that——' She broke off as a seagull swooped down and stood about a metre away from the ape's feast.

The bird waited for a moment, then slowly advanced with its head lowered in an aggressive position. At first the ape tried to ignore it, but the stare of the bright yellow eyes was too much to bear and it beat an ignominious retreat to the wall, where it turned its back and sulked. Most people laughed, but a little girl did not see it as funny.

'Oh, the poor monkey!' Her childish voice rose clearly. 'It's dreadfully upset because the nasty bird's taken its food!'

She darted from her mother, a tiny figure in a scarlet sun-dress, and approached the ape confidently. In a moment she was stroking the broad brown head and murmuring words of comfort.

For a few seconds the ape did not trouble itself to do anything about the unwanted attention. Then, suddenly, it whirled round with a snarl and dug its teeth into the child's arm. As she started to scream it leapt lightly up on to the wall, where it remained chattering angrily.

The little girl's shriek of terror and pain was echoed by her mother, and suddenly the small space was in total confusion. People exclaimed, milled about, offered advice, and generally got in the way. Thrusting his way through them with Tracy close behind, Andrew managed to reach the mother, who was almost in tears herself.

'Excuse me, I'm a doctor,' he said quietly. 'May I see the wound, please?'

Wordlessly, she held out the small forearm, from which blood was now dripping. He took it carefully and wiped it with a clean handkerchief.

'I've got a first aid kit in the car, Tracy.' He thrust the keys at her. 'Fetch it for me, please.'

As she sped away to do his bidding, she wondered what would happen now. Obviously the child needed medical attention. Was there a casualty department at the hospital?

Andrew confirmed this when she returned, and began to question the mother while he put a temporary dressing on the wounded arm. Her name, she said, was Mrs Norris, and the child was called Emma. They had been sharing a taxi with four other people from their hotel.

'I'll drive you to the hospital,' Andrew said, 'and you can get a taxi back to your hotel. Please don't worry, Mrs Norris. The wound may need a few stitches, but it's not really deep and will soon heal. The important thing is for it to be cleansed thoroughly, and for Emma to have an injection which will prevent further trouble.'

After consulting her watch, Tracy decided she had time to go with them. She was eager to see the civilian hospital where Andrew was acting orthopaedic consultant, and she looked at it with interest as they drove towards it up Hospital Hill. Like the military one, it was an elegant building, though much larger, and the casualty department was bright and attractive.

Andrew carried the child in and handed her over to a smiling nurse.

'I can't thank you enough——' Mrs Norris began.

'Please don't bother. I'm glad I happened to be on the spot.' To Tracy he added as they got into the car, 'You see how dangerous it can be to try and make pets of the apes?'

'There's no need to rub it in, and in any case I didn't feel the slightest urge to stroke one. They're not nearly as attractive as some I've seen at the Zoo.' She glanced at him as he drove down the hill. 'I think I ought to go straight back now, Andrew.'

'If you say so.'

As they returned through the narrow, busy streets, it seemed to Tracy that all the magic had gone out of the afternoon. It had been so wonderful—she had to admit it—and Andrew had revealed a side of his personality she had barely glimpsed before.

Now he had changed again, and the light-hearted friendliness had vanished. It might be because he was concentrating on threading a way through people and traffic; on the other hand, perhaps he had got tired of his self-appointed role of guide.

Next time she went sightseeing, she decided, she would go by herself and explore the little town and its shops. She might even take the Mini. After all, if Donna could manage it a girl at least five years older and that much more experienced ought to be capable of it, even in Gibraltar.

But hadn't Andrew said something about taking her to some caves on a future occasion? He'd probably forgotten already, but, in any case, she wasn't very fond of caves, so it wouldn't be of the slightest importance if he never mentioned it again.

'You'll come in and have a cup of tea, won't you?' she asked outside the house.

'I'll come in and say hello to Nerina.' He swung his long legs out of the car. 'Is the physio coming regularly as I ordered?'

'Oh, yes, and I think she's doing some good.'

'We'll give the treatment another week and then consider letting her sit up for a little while. After that the next step will be allowing her to dangle her legs over the edge of the bed.'

Tracy left him to pass on the information to his patient and went to the kitchen to make tea. It was the cook's afternoon off and Gabriella, the maid, had very little idea of making tea with boiling water.

When she returned she found Andrew sitting on the edge of the bed and Nerina radiant.

'Have you heard the good news?' she exclaimed. 'I'm really making progress!'

'Super!' Tracy squeezed round the end of the bed and put her tray on the sideboard. 'You won't be needing me much longer,' she added, and did not realise how forlorn she sounded.

'Of course I shall. I don't suppose I shall feel like doing anything for ages.'

'You'll have to go very carefully indeed,' Andrew warned her, 'but——' he hesitated '—I shouldn't be doing my duty if I didn't agree that you won't require a private nurse much longer. Say a couple of weeks.'

Pouring the tea, Tracy kept her eyes on the cups and hoped her expression was as deadpan as it felt. When she came to Gibraltar she had not looked farther into the future than the next week or so. She was well aware that modern methods of treatment did not favour keeping a patient lying prone longer than absolutely necessary.

'I want Tracy to stay as long as possible,' Nerina insisted. 'She might like to do a bit of exploring in the neighbourhood of Gib—like Tangier and Malaga.'

'I'm not supposed to be here for sightseeing!' Tracy managed to laugh and treat it lightly, but inside she was seriously concerned about the unfairness of expecting Charles to continue to pay her salary after she had ceased earning it.

On the other hand, of course, she had not got this job through the agency, so she could work for a reduced rate if she liked, or even no salary at all.

She broached the subject at the first opportunity. Donna had gone out after putting Jamie to bed, and Nerina was listening to a radio programme, so Tracy and Charles were alone in the drawing-room.

'I don't know how long you expected me to stay,' she began carefully, only to be interrupted.

'Just as long as Nerina needs you.'

'The point is—she won't need me much longer. Andrew said she could start getting up in about another week and after that a trained nurse will be really quite unnecessary. She'll have Donna, and two servants, and you——'

'Last but not least,' he put in.

'Exactly, so how could she possibly need me as well?' In some embarrassment, she added, 'I'm very conscious of being a horrible expense.'

Charles put down his coffee-cup with a bang.

'Come off it, Tracy! You know damn well I don't grudge a single penny.'

'I never supposed you did, but I don't feel happy about it, all the same.'

He glowered at her, then asked if she had discussed it with his wife.

'I said something about not being needed much longer in front of Andrew and he agreed, but Nerina said she wanted me to stay indefinitely.'

'There you are, then!' He waved a large hand and the fair hairs on the back gleamed in the lamplight. 'You've got your answer,' he added triumphantly.

Far from satisfied, Tracy sipped her coffee and considered her next move. Men hated you to think they weren't capable of spending lavishly, even in these days—specially men like Charles. But it was clear that money had got to be discussed, whether he liked it or not.

'How about a compromise?' she suggested. 'I'll leave things as they are until Nerina reaches the stage of being at least a little mobile. Then I'll remain for—say—another two weeks without any salary at all——'

'No, no!' he broke in. 'I wouldn't agree to that for a moment.'

'Hang on a minute—I hadn't finished. My idea is that I'd make it a holiday. There's a lot I'd like to see around here, but I'd be available to help Nerina if I was needed. How does that strike you?'

To her relief he appeared to be giving it serious consideration.

'It's not a bad idea,' he admitted after a while, 'if it's OK by you, but we'd better keep it a private arrangement between you and me and not mention it to my wife——'

He broke off as a piercing scream rang through the house. 'Good God—what on earth is that?'

Tracy did not stay to speculate. The sound had come from the kitchen and she was there within seconds, staring in dismay at what appeared to be a scene of utter chaos. Gabriella lay on the floor, still screaming, with an overturned stool across her legs and numerous pieces of broken plates surrounding her. More sinister, there was also a kettle lying on its side and water everywhere.

Was it hot or cold? Tracy did not need to ask, for the maid's noisy distress had already turned to sobs and she held up one arm with an angry red patch appearing on it.

Maria, the cook, was jabbering excitedly in Spanish, but Tracy ignored her and gave her full attention to Gabriella. It seemed unlikely there had been any serious damage done and it was important that the scalded arm should be put under the cold water tap as quickly as possible.

'The stool——' Maria had switched to English. 'It fall over when she stand on it!'

Gabriella must have been getting some plates off a top shelf, Tracy deduced, and had lost her balance, knocking the kettle over as she fell. Hastily she removed the stool and helped the maid to her feet. Before Gabriella knew what was happening, she was holding her arm firmly under a stream of cold water.

There were more shrieks from the patient, and cries of horror from the cook, but Tracy persisted in her treatment. She didn't think it was a bad scald, but it would be painful for a time, and considerably more so without the cooling effect of the water.

Gradually the turmoil in the kitchen subsided and Maria began cheerfully to clear up the mess while Tracy put a light bandage on the injured arm. She would have liked to leave it exposed to the air, but Gabriella was so proud of the adornment that she felt it was probably worth it psychologically.

'What was all that about?' asked Nerina when her nurse returned to duty. She listened in mingled concern and amusement to Tracy's account, then commented, 'What a good thing you were here to take charge, otherwise it would have taken Gabriella the rest of the day to calm down.'

Tracy laughed and began to give Nerina an edited account of her interrupted conversation with Charles. The following day, with a view to preparing herself for her 'holiday', she drove the Mini to the shops and spent a happy two hours exploring the town. This became the pattern for the next few days, and on returning from one of these expeditions she was surprised and delighted to find her patient sitting up in bed with the physiotherapist in charge.

'Mr Lincoln gave permission.' The girl, who was a Gibraltarian with dark Spanish looks, smiled proudly. 'It is a big step forward, yes?'

'Terrific,' Tracy agreed. 'When can she sit on the edge of the bed?'

'You'll have to ask him, but perhaps tomorrow or the next day.'

After the physiotherapist had left Nerina demanded to be told why she had to have special permission for the next stage. 'Dangling my legs over the edge seems such a simple thing,' she pointed out.

'You used to be a nurse,' Tracy reminded her. 'Don't you remember how strange patients always feel having their legs bent after keeping them straight for some time? You're quite likely to be dizzy.'

'Oh, I hope not—I absolutely hate it when things start going round and round. It was like that when I came round after getting concussion.' Nerina picked up a magazine which Tracy had bought in the town. 'You *will* phone Andrew, won't you?'

For some reason Tracy was reluctant to perform this simple task, but she duly did so the following day.

'Great!' he exclaimed when she told him there had been no ill effects of being allowed to sit up. 'I'll be along to see her tomorrow.'

Nerina greeted him with a radiant smile, and he

spent some time carefully moving her legs from one position to another and asking searching questions.

'No pain in your back when I do this—or this?'

'None at all.' Honestly, she added, 'It feels a bit funny, though.'

'It's bound to do that, and you must be very careful not to overdo it. Your muscles won't be much use at first.' He stood considering her thoughtfully, then suddenly smiled. 'Right, you can try your edge-of-the-bed act.'

Tracy helped her slide to the edge and cautiously lower her legs. Her feet hung just clear of the floor and she swung them experimentally.

'You'll have to lower the bed before I can stand,' she said to Tracy, but it was Andrew who answered.

'You're not doing that today.' His eyes twinkled at Tracy's deadpan expression. 'I wouldn't mind betting the bed was left high purposely just in case you got venturesome.'

'When can I try walking?' Nerina demanded.

'Maybe tomorrow, if you feel up to it. But it might be as well to wait until your husband can be here. He's a big strong chap.'

'You're not anticipating he'll be needed?'

'No, no—just being cautious, that's all.' He looked Tracy up and down, and she was glad she wasn't wearing her shorts. 'I'm quite sure *you* wouldn't have the strength to pick up a patient off the floor.'

She flushed indignantly. 'I wouldn't need to! I'd take good care no patient of mine ever landed on the floor.' Seeing the smile in his eyes, she knew she had overreacted. 'Anyway, I'm a lot stronger than I look. Most nurses are.'

Later, when she was escorting him out to his car just like the sister on a ward, he asked her about the future.

'Have you solved your problem about whether to stay on a bit longer?'

'Yes, thank you. Charles and I came to an arrangement and I'm going to spend a couple of weeks having a sort of holiday. That way I can help Nerina whenever she needs it.'

'A very good idea. There's a great deal you haven't seen yet.' Andrew paused with his hand on the door handle. 'I promised to take you to see St Michael's Cave.'

'Oh—er—did you?'

'Whether I did or not doesn't really matter. I'm asking you now. How about Wednesday afternoon?'

Tracy's heart was behaving rather oddly, but she managed to answer with cool politeness. 'I think that would be all right.'

Afterwards she wondered why she hadn't told him she didn't like caves.

CHAPTER FOUR

THE day that Nerina walked to the window, Charles brought champagne home to be drunk at supper, regardless of the fact that his wife would still be taking her meal in her room.

Donna wrinkled her nose when she was given a glass and complained it tasted 'funny', but Tracy noticed she accepted a refill, with the result that she staggered when she got up from the table and giggled hysterically.

'You've made me tiddly,' she accused him.

'I didn't force you to drink it,' he pointed out. 'Better ask Maria to give you some black coffee.'

'I shan't sleep if I have that.'

'Please yourself.' He laughed and tweaked a handful of her long hair.

Tracy was only half listening to their banter. She was feeling unaccountably happy and she supposed it must be the effect of the champagne. It couldn't possibly be anything to do with the fact that she was going out with Andrew tomorrow.

She was still in a contented frame of mind when she went to bed, and she lay for a little while thinking about the weeks she had spent in Gibraltar. By rights, she should be turning her thoughts towards departure, and she experienced a glow of satisfaction because she didn't need to do that just yet. Dreamily she turned her attention to planning what she should do when she was officially free of her nursing job. Maybe, after a while, Nerina would be well enough to go out with her in the Mini. They would have a wonderful time. . .

Two hours later she was wide awake again. Some small sound had disturbed her, but for a moment she couldn't think what it was. Then it was repeated, and this time she recognised it at once—the half-asleep, fretful cry of a restless child.

Jamie, she remembered, had seemed slightly out of sorts during the day, but no one had regarded it as being of any consequence. Perhaps his little tummy was uncomfortable and Donna would go to him and administer a dose of something. Wide awake now, Tracy listened for a soft step on the landing, but heard nothing. Eventually she got up and quietly opened her bedroom door.

Donna's door was ajar, which made it all the more strange that she didn't seem to have heard the child.

At that moment Jamie cried out again, and without further hesitation Tracy crossed to his room and went in.

'What's the matter, love?' She leaned over the cot and, by the light of the low-powered bulb he always had on at night, saw a flushed face and watery eyes.

The child was undoubtedly feverish and had been tossing about judging by the state of the bed.

Tracy debated whether she ought to take his temperature, but decided it was unnecessary. Talking in a soothing whisper, she scooped him up and, with her free hand, smoothed the bottom sheet and tucked it in firmly.

'Drink,' Jamie murmured and, looking round, she saw bottled water and a mug on a shelf over the washbasin.

As she moved across the room an exclamation from behind her caused her to glance round. Donna stood in the doorway, a loose négligé held carelessly round her naked body. Strangely, she too was looking flushed and with over-bright eyes.

'What on earth do you think you're doing?' she burst out. 'Jamie is my responsibility, not yours.'

'I waited for you to come to him when he first cried out,' Tracy said calmly, 'but when you didn't I thought I'd better investigate. He seems to have a slight fever, so perhaps it would be a good idea to dose him with whatever you usually use.'

'If you say so. You're the medical boss around here,' Donna said rudely.

She almost snatched the child from Tracy's arms, and he immediately snuggled into her shoulder. Pushing the hair back from his hot little face, she murmured words of love and comfort.

There was absolutely no doubt about her love for her little charge, Tracy reflected, and she looked after him well. Which made it all the more strange that she had not come when he cried.

'I'll leave you to cope,' she said calmly. 'I hope Jamie's OK in the morning.'

It was dark on the landing and she paused to get her bearings. As her eyes adjusted to the faint light coming from the window, she saw something which caused her to halt in astonishment and shock.

The nanny's door was still ajar, exactly as she had seen it earlier, but Charles's door was open—not wide but just enough to allow the passage of a slim body. Donna?

Remembering the flushed face and brilliant eyes, the overreaction to finding someone else had taken charge, Tracy nevertheless tried hard to convince herself she was mistaken in her suspicion. She couldn't bear to think that Charles—whom she liked and had once very nearly fallen in love with—was actually being unfaithful to his wife while she lay almost helpless in bed downstairs.

Yet Donna was very attractive in a sexy sort of way and quite often flirted with him openly, though Tracy had to admit he had not given her much encouragement. Not in front of other people, at any rate. Unfortunately there was no knowing what he did in private.

On the verge of regaining her room, she paused. It was extremely probable that Nerina was awake and worrying about Jamie. She ought to go downstairs and explain.

As she had guessed, she found her patient wide awake and restless.

'I heard Jamie the first time,' Nerina whispered. 'Why was Donna so slow about going to him?'

'I think she was very sound asleep. It was the champagne, I expect—she's not used to it,' Tracy explained.

'Could be. What was the trouble?'

'He seems a bit feverish, but nothing to worry about. Didn't he go to a party about ten days ago? Could be he's picked up something. There are still a few childish complaints that aren't inoculated against, but they aren't important.' Tracy changed the subject. 'And now let me see if I can make you a bit more comfortable. Would you like one of your sleeping tablets?'

'I suppose it might be a good idea,' Nerina admitted reluctantly.

Tracy smoothed the bottom sheet and supplied a fresh cool nightdress, talking quietly about nothing very much as she did so. When the tablet had been swallowed, she checked her patient's pulse and was glad to find it already steadying. Before leaving, she found a tuneful, dreamy tape and set it playing softly.

Upstairs again, she faced the impossible task of getting to sleep herself. She managed it eventually and slept until the Spanish maid, who always arrived at seven o'clock, roused her with a cup of what she called tea.

'Thank you, Gabriella.'

Sipping sleepily, she found all the events of the night rushing back into her mind, but somehow now that the darkness had gone and the sun was shining, everything looked different. After all, she *might* have been mistaken about the position of the two bedroom doors.

So why not give Charles and Donna the benefit of the doubt?

Tracy was very anxious to do so, and it was made rather easier by another, much pleasanter thought. This afternoon she was going out with Andrew.

As she dressed she heard Jamie chattering to Donna and concluded thankfully that there didn't seem much wrong with him. At breakfast she inevitably found herself studying the nanny surreptitiously, but could detect no appearance of guilt. Charles she did not see at all, since he had left the house early.

It was obviously going to be a perfectly normal morning. Only the afternoon would be different.

St Michael's Cave was high up on the Rock but approachable by road. Before they went in Tracy debated whether to confess her fear of caves. It was a very real phobia. The narrower passages gave her claustrophobia, and when the guide switched off the lights for a moment as, in her experience guides invariably did, she had difficulty in not screaming. She had always been ashamed of this, so she decided to keep quiet about it.

She was glad she had said nothing when they got inside. It seemed that all they had to do was to walk through an immense cavern, well lit, and admire the stalactites.

'It's like a cathedral,' she said in an awestricken tone.

'It's funny you should call it that, because this part is known as Cathedral Cave, and ahead there's an even bigger space which is used for concerts. It seats a thousand people.' Andrew broke off to laugh. 'Sorry! You've got your well-informed courier back again.'

'I don't mind,' she assured him.

'No? You could have fooled me the other day. I got the impression I was boring you stiff.'

'Of course I wasn't bored! And I certainly wouldn't be by anything you could tell me in here. It's a super place.' Tracy moved on towards the steps leading to the concert area, but he put out a hand and caught her arm.

'Hang on—you haven't seen the really interesting part. The majority of tourist parties just tramp through here and think they know all about St Michael's Cave, but there's also a lower cave. Come on, let's go and explore that.'

On the verge of protest, Tracy felt her hand taken in a firm, warm clasp and allowed the words to die unspoken. If he went on holding her like that, maybe she would find the courage to go with him to the other cave without disgracing herself by an attack of panic. So she made no attempt to pull herself free, and Andrew continued to hold her hand as they made their way steadily downwards.

WIND OF CHANGE

'Shut your eyes,' he commanded suddenly. 'I want you to get the full impact.'

Obediently she lowered her lashes, and felt the weight of his arm round her shoulders, guiding her stumbling steps. She shivered, and he asked her if she was cold and drew her closer. His warmth was both a comfort and a delight to her, and when he told her to open her eyes she did so without fear.

The next moment she gave a gasp of horror.

They were standing on the brink of a vast underground lake. Dark water glimmered restlessly in the dim light and seemed to stretch into the far distance where it vanished into the greater darkness of wet rock. A small sinister wind ruffled her hair and sent a tremor all over her body so that she had difficulty in preventing her teeth from chattering.

'Wonderful, isn't it?' Andrew enthused. 'Goodness knows how deep it is, but there are the usual rumours about it having no bottom. That rather eerie little wind is supposed to come through a tunnel under the sea all the way from Africa. It's a load of rubbish, of course, but it ties in with the legend about the apes knowing about an escape route to Africa through a tunnel.'

Carried away by his intense interest, he stopped holding Tracy and stepped forward, right to the edge of that evil black water.

Her scream rang through the cave, echoing and re-echoing. Regardless of her own terror, she plunged towards him and clutched him violently by the arm.

'Come back! Andrew, *please* come back! I can't bear to see you standing so close—you might slip——'

Far from being flattered by her concern, he was annoyed. 'For heaven's sake, Tracy—I'm not that daft, I hope! And anyway, you might have made me lose my balance, grabbing me suddenly like that.'

She released her grip and he stepped back to a safer position. Turning her head, she tried to hide that she was on the verge of tears.

'I'm sorry I was so silly, but—but I don't like this kind of place and I was frightened. Can't we go up again now, Andrew, please?'

'I believe you're really upset.' He put his hands on her shoulders and looked down with concern into her face. 'If you don't like caves, why didn't you say so at the beginning, silly girl?'

'I—I thought you'd laugh at me.'

'You must have a pretty low opinion of my intelligence. I hope I can recognise a real phobia when I see it.' He drew out a handkerchief and dried the few tears she had been unable to control. 'Better now?'

'Yes, th-thank you,' she assured him breathlessly, hoping he wouldn't notice the sudden racing of her pulses.

'Perhaps we ought to make quite sure.' He slid his hands down from her shoulders and pressed them against her back, drawing her close so that her body was moulded against his. His lips were gentle at first, but as she responded instinctively, their pressure grew greater until she could no longer breathe, and she broke away with a small cry of protest.

At that moment they heard voices, sounding eerie and hollow, and a family party came into view. Two teenage boys rushed forward to the edge of the lake with excited exclamations, and Tracy felt a fresh onslaught of shame at her own cowardice.

'Time we were going.'

Andrew slipped his arm into hers and steered her towards the passage leading to the upper cave. Tracy went with him thankfully, and as they stepped into the fresh air and sunshine she found that the horror which had gripped her by the underground lake had receded into the dark recesses of her mind.

She had made a fool of herself—that was for sure—but Andrew had not seemed to mind, once he got over his astonishment, and he had comforted her in a way that was vivid in her memory so that she could still in imagination feel the sensual delight of his kiss.

'I think we'd better complete your restoration by having tea at Catalan Bay,' he said briskly as they reached the car. 'The hotel there is very spectacularly situated, looking out to sea. I think you'll like it.'

It was the first time Tracy had seen any of Gibraltar's beaches, and she was greatly attracted by the little place with its tiny village down at shore level. They had their tea on a terrace near the seawater swimming pool, shaded by a sun-umbrella which, now that summer had almost arrived, was very necessary. All round them the hotel guests disported themselves in the pool, or enjoyed their tea, or simply did nothing at all.

It was strange, Tracy reflected, that she had no feeling of being part of a crowd. It was just as though she and Andrew were on their own. Perhaps that was why she had a sudden urge to tell him about last night.

She resisted it for some time, conscious that she had no right to discuss her friends' intimate problems with an outsider.

But Andrew wasn't really an outsider. He knew everything there was to know about Nerina's body and had made some shrewd guesses concerning the state of her mind. Besides, telling a doctor wasn't quite like telling just anybody; you could at least be sure that what you said would be regarded as confidential.

'Do you remember that question about Nerina's state of mind you asked me at the hospital the first time we met?' she asked suddenly, breaking a short silence.

'Second time,' he corrected.

'What? Oh, you mean the first was on the plane when I disliked you so intensely. It doesn't count.'

'That's a relief,' he said solemnly, but his eyes were laughing at her. 'Which particular question do you mean?'

'About Nerina's relations with Charles. I wouldn't believe there could be anything wrong, and I went on believing it after she came home.' She paused to take a sip of tea. 'Until last night.' As briefly and objectively as possible she told him what had occurred.

He listened without interruption, his eyes on his plate. When she had finished he said only, 'Pity.'

'*Pity*? Is that all you've got to say?' Tracy exclaimed. 'If my suspicion is true, a better word to use would be *tragedy*!'

'Of course it's not a tragedy. You're exaggerating the importance of it absurdly. You're grown up, Tracy, don't you realise that sort of thing happens all the time?'

The question brought her up with a jerk. Of course she realised it. She ought to, with a sister who was divorced and a brother whose numerous girlfriends had probably included married ones. But she hadn't wanted it to happen to Nerina and Charles. Their marriage had seemed so happy and safe, until the accident.

'You sounded as though you thought it didn't matter,' she said slowly, 'yet when Nerina was in hospital you were sufficiently concerned because you thought she was worried to let her go home. That doesn't make sense to me.'

'I never said the possibility of Charles having it

off with the nanny didn't matter,' Andrew protested. 'I only meant you were exaggerating the seriousness of it.'

Sensing that he hadn't finished, Tracy fixed puzzled eyes on his face and waited. An extra-loud splash, followed by a shriek, from the pool momentarily caught her attention, but no one seemed to be drowning, and their surroundings again faded into a blur of heat and colour.

'Charles is obviously a virile man with strong sexual feelings, and the girl is a sexy little creature,' Andrew went on thoughtfully. 'If she offered what he was in need of, it's only natural he should accept it, but I'm sure it meant nothing. Besides, we don't even know they had anything more than a kiss and cuddle. *If* any of it happened at all.'

'Are you telling me a man with strong sexual impulses isn't required to be faithful to his wife?' Outraged, Tracy fixed him with a truculent stare. 'That's a positively Victorian idea, when they had one set of values for the man and another for the woman——'

'Of course I didn't mean that.'

'But you implied it.' She whipped up her indignation and swept on. 'I think it's disgustingly sexist——'

'So you think the woman should have the same freedom?' He held up a hand to halt her immediate protest. 'But, Tracy love, surely in these days she has?'

Wallowing in deep waters, she could feel herself

sinking. They were supposed to be talking about Charles and Donna, weren't they? So how did they get on to the subject of marriage in general?

'The best thing you can do,' Andrew was advising when she managed to get her concentration back, 'is to forget all about what *may* have happened and give all your energies to getting Nerina back to normal as soon as possible. You're doing a grand job there, so keep up the good work.'

'I shall do my best to obey your instructions,' she said woodenly.

He raised his eyebrows and looked at her quizzically, and suddenly they were both laughing.

'Thank you for showing me the caves.' She picked up her bag. 'They were—very interesting, but I think I ought to be getting back now.'

'You've got time to pour me another cup of tea first,' he said calmly, holding out his cup.

That evening Tracy heard her name being called from the direction of the bathroom, and when she went to investigate she found Donna staring in dismay at Jamie's back.

'I thought he was sickening for something last night, and he's been grumpy all day, which isn't like him at all.' Her greenish eyes fastened imploringly on Tracy's face. 'Do say it isn't anything serious!'

'Most unlikely.' Tracy bent to look closely at the bare back and discovered a group of small spots. 'I should think it's probably chickenpox and he may have caught it at the party he went to. But there's nothing to worry about. He's very likely already over the worst, though he'll get a lot more spots.'

'*Chickenpox?*' The nanny could not have sounded more alarmed if smallpox had been mentioned. 'That's a horrible complaint! You get the most disgusting spots and they irritate dreadfully, but you musn't scratch them or you get scarred for life.'

'You've had it, then?' queried Tracy.

'No, I haven't, and I don't want to get it either. It would be an absolute disaster!'

Tracy glanced at the clear tanned skin and repressed an uncharitable desire to see it covered in ugly spots. 'If you've escaped so far you may not catch it now, but there's nothing you can do about it, so I shouldn't worry if I were you.'

'How can I help worrying?' Donna automatically retrieved a plastic duck from the floor and handed it back to its owner. 'I most particularly didn't want to risk anything just now, because of the June Ball.'

On the verge of departure, Tracy paused to ask casually, 'What's that?'

'Hasn't Nerina mentioned it? Oh, well, I suppose she's not very interested this year since she won't be able to go. It's an absolutely super affair at the Barracks. The Commanding Officer invites all his officers to a special dinner in the mess, and then afterwards there's dancing.'

Tracy absorbed the information with more care

than she had displayed hitherto. Donna had not appeared to have a military boyfriend, but presumably somebody had invited her, and that might mean—*should* mean— her suspicions last night were unfounded.

'Are you expecting to go?' she asked.

Donna lifted a protesting child from the bath and wrapped him in a big towel on her lap. 'I'm certainly hoping to go, though I haven't exactly got an invitation *yet*.'

Tracy waited, sensing that there was more to come, and Donna was torn between a wish to show off and a feeling that it might be better to keep quiet.

Eventually the girl burst out, 'I think it's quite likely Charles will take me instead of Nerina.'

Receiving no reply, she looked up with an air of defiance, and Tracy pulled herself together.

'What makes you think that?'

'Just something he said about me having rather a dull time while Nerina's been ill and he'd have to see what he could do to make up for it. She used to look after Jamie quite a lot and I had plenty of free time. I think they only have me so they don't need to bother with getting babysitters when they want to go out. Army people have a terrific social life.'

Donna broke off and looked closely at the child's back. 'Here's another spot—and another! I shall *die* if I get chickenpox before the Ball! Oh, Tracy, isn't there anything I can do to ward it off?'

'Nothing whatsoever,' Tracy told her, and hoped she hadn't sounded too pleased about it.

But Donna was too absorbed in her own fears to notice.

CHAPTER FIVE

TRACY watched her patient's increasing mobility with mixed feelings. Once she suggested the time had now come for her to stop being a professional nurse on a job, and start her two weeks' holiday, but Nerina strenuously resisted it.

'Wait until I start going out in the car. I'd love it if you could be here to drive me at first. Charles wouldn't think much of taking me on short excursions at a sedate speed, and though Donna's quite a nice girl she's so *young*. I don't find her a very stimulating companion when Charles isn't at home.' She re-settled the cushion at her back and finished triumphantly, 'Anyway, you can't leave Gilbraltar until after the June Ball.'

'Why can't I?' queried Tracy.

'Hasn't Charles told you?'

'Not a word.' Feigning uninterest, Tracy flicked over the pages of the magazine on her lap.

'Isn't that just like a man! He intends to take you instead of me, that's all. You'll love it, Tracy—it's the great social event of the year, as far as the military is concerned, I mean. I just can't think why he hasn't mentioned it.'

Perhaps because he was planning to take Donna? Tracy still couldn't believe it was likely to happen, but it was impossible not to feel slightly uneasy.

'I couldn't possibly go, Nerina,' she pointed out. 'For one thing, I haven't anything to wear. Nurses don't take ballgowns with them when they take jobs abroad.'

'There's plenty of time to get one, and it would be cheaper than in the UK because of there being no VAT. I'd love to go with you to choose a dress, but I couldn't face it yet.'

'I should think not!' Tracy hesitated, then added tentatively, 'But you might manage to attend the dinner.'

'How did you know there was a dinner?' asked Nerina.

She couldn't possibly say, 'Donna told me,' after pretending ignorance of the whole thing, so she merely answered in a casual tone, 'Don't these affairs usually start with a dinner?'

'Well, yes, quite often, and this one certainly does, but I couldn't possibly go. I still feel terribly shaky, and it would be a real ordeal with everybody asking me how I am and making a lot of fuss. Charles wouldn't want to go without a partner, so you'll just have to take my place.' Rather disconsolately, Nerina added, 'I thought you'd be thrilled.'

'Oh, I am! I wish you were going to be there too, that's all.' Tracy got up with sudden resolution. 'It's time I was getting you to bed.'

'I shall miss all this spoiling when you've gone home,' Nerina mourned.

'I'm not going just yet, and by the time I do leave you won't need any waiting on.'

Later, when she was saying goodnight, Tracy paused in the doorway. 'Do remind that husband of yours that I can't partner him if I haven't received a proper invitation from the person most concerned. No girl likes being asked to a ball by proxy!'

Nerina laughed. 'He'll be late back tonight, but I'll get on to him first thing in the morning, I promise.'

After a late night on duty, Charles was pottering about at home most of the morning, but Tracy waited in vain for her invitation. It was not until he and she were alone in the drawing-room after lunch that he suddenly introduced the subject.

'Nerina's been tearing me off a strip for not inviting you officially to the June Ball.' He grinned at her disarmingly. 'Sorry about that. I'm afraid I thought you'd take it for granted I'd take you instead of her.'

'I didn't know anything about it until last week when Donna happened to mention it,' Tracy told him.

She glanced at him from beneath her lashes but could detect no sign of embarrassment. He was lolling back in his chair, looking more like a holidaymaker in his open-necked shirt than an officer in the Army. His arms and hands were deeply tanned and his light hair bleached almost white.

There was virility in every line of him, and she once more felt thankful she was now immune to it.

'I expect Donna wishes some unattached young officer would invite her,' he said lazily. 'Can I take it you've accepted the invitation, Tracy?'

'Was that what it was?' She laughed. 'All right, Charles, I'll be your partner, since you're so pressing, and after that I shall have to tear up my roots and depart to England.'

'It's nice to know you feel you've put down roots here,' he said.

Tracy shook her head. 'Putting down roots in my sort of job is *not* a good idea. Pulling them up is apt to be painful.'

It would be far more painful to leave than she would have thought possible, and it wasn't because she was so fond of Nerina. Gibraltar had put chains on her heart, and she knew she would feel the weight for some time.

'I'm glad you've been happy with us.' Charles smiled at her and consulted his watch. 'I must be going. See you!'

When Nerina woke up from the afternoon nap she still found necessary, Tracy gave her an edited report on her conversation with her husband.

'So now I haven't any excuse for not buying that dress,' she went on. 'I'll find out when Donna doesn't need the car and——'

'You're to take it whether she needs it or not!' Nerina's voice had sharpened suddenly. 'She's had it almost entirely to herself since my fall.'

Tracy did not argue, and the following afternoon she drove carefully down to the shopping area, and managed to park not far from Main Street. The little town was crowded, as usual, with tourists who wandered in and out of the shops, exclaiming at the prices.

'This would be thirty pounds in Regent Street,' she heard one woman say, 'and here it's only five!'

She was fingering one of the numerous shawls, both gauzy and woollen, which hung outside a shop. Tracy had bought one soon after she arrived and considered it one of the best buys in the whole of Main Street. It would do nicely to put round her shoulders after the Ball, when the temperature dropped.

She wandered on, staring into the shop windows and sometimes going inside to try dresses on. Eventually she fell for a slinky dress in green and gold wild silk, with an off-the-shoulder neckline. The colour suited her tan and picked up the golden lights in her hair, and it fitted perfectly.

The Indian shopkeeper exclaimed that it might have been made for her and, seizing his opportunity, produced some shoes to go with it. Tracy paid for both with a feeling of gay abandon, and departed well satisfied with her afternoon.

As she drove home she wondered whether Donna knew of the invitation. Or was she still hoping for one herself?

The question was destined to remain unanswered. That evening the nanny developed chickenpox, and she looked so ill that Tracy ordered her to stay in bed for a couple of days.

'I'll look after Jamie,' she offered. 'I shall enjoy it.'

The little boy had rapidly got over his shyness when she first arrived and appeared willing to accept her as a substitute for his beloved Donna. In particular Tracy loved bathing him, and willingly put up with being splashed for the sake of the cuddle which followed while she dried him.

At the end of the two days Donna returned to her duties. Apart from her spots—which were every bit as ugly as she had feared—she seemed to have recovered.

'I can't possibly go to the Ball now,' she said in tragic tones when she happened to be alone with Tracy. 'Did you ever know such filthy luck!'

Commiserating with her, Tracy felt glad the question had not been answered. In her own mind she could give Charles the benefit of the doubt and—which was much more important—Nerina would never know that her husband had ever contemplated taking the nanny to the Ball. If he really had, which she still thought unlikely.

Although Tracy had been looking forward to the June Ball, she dressed for it with an odd feeling of depression. Yet, looking at herself in the long mirror, she couldn't help feeling pleased with her appearance. The gold necklace with long matching earrings went perfectly with the dress, and the shampoo she had given herself that afternoon had been particularly successful. Her soft gleaming hair fell to her shoulders and framed a face which had been made up with great care, using a new lipstick and eye-shadow. Everything, she decided, was most satisfactory.

Everything except her mood. The grey eyes should have been brilliant with excitement, her lips curving in a smile of happy anticipation, and neither was making the slightest attempt to do anything of the sort. So what was wrong?

Not daring to probe into her emotions in case of what she might find, she picked up the evening bag which Nerina had lent her, along with the necklace and earrings, and went in search of Charles. She found him in his wife's room, and made no attempt to repress a gasp of admiration. Tall and broad-shouldered, he was magnificent in his dress uniform, and she wished she felt capable of appreciating him as he deserved.

She did her best and said lightly, 'You look absolutely stupendous, Charles! A partner any girl could be proud of.'

'I'm glad you realise your luck, Tracy.' He grinned and looked her up and down. 'If I may say so, you're looking rather special yourself.'

Nerina made an exclamation of disgust. 'For goodness' sake take this mutual admiration society off to the Ball and let me have a bit of peace! I've got a new novel I'm longing to start.'

As they left the house, Charles said soberly,

'She's putting a brave face on it, but I reckon she feels bloody awful inside. She's always enjoyed dressing up and dancing and all that sort of thing.'

'She'll be able to do it again before long if she keeps up the present rate of progress,' Tracy assured him.

'We've got a lot to thank you for.' He took her hand and squeezed it.

'You've got nothing at all,' she protested. 'It was the physio and the orthopaedist and her own determination——'

'And you.'

They argued about it amicably during the short drive to the Officers' Mess, where they joined a long line of people waiting to shake hands with the hosts for the evening. Colonel and Mrs Hamilton were both tall and grey-haired, the man even more resplendent than Charles and his lady dignified in stiff moiré silk in a deep maroon shade which clashed badly with her flushed face. Looking at her with a professional eye, Tracy decided she probably had high blood pressure, or perhaps even heart trouble.

Dinner was preceded by a reception at which the guests circulated and sipped sherry served by soldiers. Everyone seemed to know everyone else, and the hum of conversation was unceasing. Charles was momentarily detained by a fellow officer, and Tracy, reflecting that Donna wouldn't have cared much for this part, stood alone by a small table holding nuts and canapés.

Very much aware of being a stranger in their midst, she was feeling a little out of it, though nothing of that showed in her expression as she allowed her eyes to drift slowly over the colourful and animated crowd. Suddenly she stiffened, the background noise faded and her gaze remained fixed on one particular guest.

A tall, dark man, not in uniform.

He had his back turned and was talking to a pretty woman possibly in her thirties, who looked up at him with flattering attention. She was small, not even reaching his shoulder, and her low-cut dress of some filmy white material was dramatic with her deep tan and bright corn-coloured hair.

She was just as much a stranger to Tracy as the other people at the reception, but the man with her was not a stranger at all. As he turned slightly and she saw his face, she knew with a cold, sick dread that it was Andrew.

Shocked at the violence of her reaction, Tracy took herself sternly to task. He had as much right to be with a strange woman as she had to partner Charles. And if she had imagined he had any special interest in herself, then she must be out of her mind. He had enjoyed showing her Gibraltar because he was fond of the place, and for no other reason.

Charles came back and apologised for leaving her alone. They both accepted a second glass of sherry and, shortly afterwards, went in to dinner.

The Mess was beautifully decorated with flowering plants and a small string band played discreetly in an alcove. The long tables had flower arrangements and tall candles at mathematically regular intervals, the tablecloths were whiter than white, the cutlery and glasses shone and the place cards had been beautifully executed by an expert in calligraphy. It was a glittering scene, and Tracy firmly banished Andrew and his companion to the back of her mind and absorbed it with interest and appreciation.

Unfortunately she could still see him. He was not at all near, but by some freak of fate there was a clear, though narrow, passage which led straight through the nodding heads of the diners from her to him. Not that he ever looked in Tracy's direction, but his lack of awareness made her feel free to allow her eyes to drift that way far too often for her peace of mind.

Eventually she said casually to Charles, 'I thought I noticed Andrew Lincoln with someone. Surely the men here are supposed to be all military?'

'Any bloke who gets invited by a female who's without her normal partner can certainly come. Who was he with?'

'How would I know?' Tracy pretended to pause for thought. 'She was fair and small and quite attractive.'

'Not much doubt about her, then. I reckon it was Angela Grayson. Major Grayson hates this sort of function and most conveniently picked up some sort of summer 'flu bug.' Charles lowered his voice. 'I don't suppose Angela was averse to a change of partner.'

Tracy made no comment, and for the remainder of the meal they both gave most of their attention to their neighbours. Tracy's was a young lieutenant with red hair who turned out to be so amusing she was able to forget the jolt which Andrew's presence had given her. His name was Clive, he told her, and when the dancing began later on he attached himself to her.

Since Charles much preferred to prop up the bar and talk shop with his friends, Tracy had no objection. It was with Clive that she was dancing when she came face to face with Andrew.

Apparently he had not noticed her before. There was a startled look in his eyes when they met hers over his petite partner's head, and she flung him a dazzling smile, at the same time entirely losing the thread of her own partner's conversation.

Andrew made a slight formal inclination of the head but did not return the smile, but she saw him dart a look at her partner.

'Is something wrong?' asked Clive, sensing he had lost her attention.

'No, of course not. I just happened to see someone I knew.'

The next dance was a waltz, perhaps included in the programme specially for the older people. Tracy was not surprised when her partner apologised for being unable to face tackling it, and resigned herself to sitting on the sidelines and watching. The floor gradually filled up, and Angela Grayson came whirling past in the arms of the Colonel, who appeared to be hugely enjoying himself.

Tracy looked after them a little wistfully. The lovely sensual music was doing something to her senses and her whole body yearned to dip and sway in time to it.

'May I have the pleasure?' a man's voice said suddenly, and she jerked round to find Andrew standing before her, holding out his arm with old-fashioned courtesy.

She rose without a word and slipped into his embrace as if she had been waiting for just that moment. Perhaps she had, she thought dreamily, perhaps she had known instinctively that he would come, or had she only hoped he might? Whatever the truth, it didn't matter. The important thing was that he *had* come, and for a few minutes he was hers.

Still silent, they revolved slowly, their bodies moving in a perfect unison which sent her pulses racing. She could feel the warmth of his hand on her back and the pressure of his fingers as they gently and unobtrusively caressed her flesh beneath the thin silk. As the lights were dimmed he bent his head and rested his cheek against her hair.

'You smell nice,' he said softly.

'Do I?' was all she could think of to say in reply.

Shutting her eyes, she drifted on a flood of emotion. If only the languorous music would go on and on. . . if only they could go on dancing like this until the evening ended . . .

She forgot about Charles and Angela Grayson. She remembered only that she was leaving Gibraltar soon and this might be the last time she would ever see Andrew. She would take away with her the memory of him, his good looks and lean, hard body, and the feel of him in her arms, and then she would try to forget. He would become just another little bit of experience, but unfortunately rather more painful than some.

The lights came up and the music stopped.

'You dance very well,' Andrew said politely.

'So do you.'

'Are you deputising for Nerina?'

'Yes.'

He was still holding her hand as he glanced round for two empty chairs. When he spotted a space and drew her towards it she went with him without hesitation.

'I hope she's still progressing well,' he remarked as they sat down.

'Yes,' Tracy said again, feeling an utter idiot. Making an effort, she added, 'I suppose she's no longer one of your patients?'

'She's certainly not in need of any more visits.' Andrew hesitated, then asked, 'Have you stopped worrying about the nanny?'

She remembered how lightly he had treated her

concern and stiffened slightly. 'I haven't had any reason to worry. The poor girl's got chickenpox at the moment and——' She broke off hastily.

Angela Grayson had appeared in front of them.

'So there you are, darling!' Her large blue eyes flickered over Tracy. She lowered her voice. 'I thought I'd never escape from that old bore. Do buy me a drink to cheer me up.'

Andrew stood up at once. 'Can I get you anything?' he asked courteously, glancing casually down at Tracy with the naturalness of a man who prided himself on good manners.

'No, thank you.' She smiled brilliantly at them both. 'I'll just sit here until Charles remembers my existence.'

But as soon as they had gone she felt a sudden need for escape, and the only possible place was the ladies' cloakroom. She would be unlikely to be alone there, but at least she wouldn't have to talk to anybody unless she wanted to.

There were only two women there when she entered. One was an exceedingly plain girl, expensively dressed, who Charles had told her was a niece of Colonel Hamilton, visiting from England. The other was the Colonel's wife, and both were busy at the mirror.

Ignoring them, Tracy opened her bag and began to attend to her face, using the mirror on the opposite wall. She worked mechanically, reliving in her mind the ecstasy of that dance with Andrew. Why on earth had she been such a fool as to let herself get carried away like that? At her age she really ought not to be so vulnerable to soft music and dim lights, and the feel of an attractive man's arms round her.

A sudden exclamation behind her caused her to spin round just in time to see Mrs Hamilton clutch the back of a chair, her florid face greenish-white and her lips blue. She swayed dangerously, and the niece made an ineffectual grab at her. Before Tracy could leap to her assistance, the big woman slid to the floor and lay in an ungainly heap, completely unconscious.

Already suspecting a heart attack, Tracy went down on her knees. 'Quick!' she said urgently to the white-faced girl. 'Go and fetch the tall dark man who isn't in uniform. He's a doctor—*hurry!*'

Left alone, Tracy could detect no pulse or sign of breathing. Automatically, without stopping to speculate on the chances of success, she started resuscitation. For what seemed an eternity there was no sound in the ladies' cloakroom but her own steady breathing, in and out, in and out, filling the patient's lungs with air.

Suddenly she was alone no longer. Andrew was there, kneeling beside her. He said tersely, 'OK Tracy, I'll take over,' and directed a fierce blow to Mrs Hamilton's diaphragm, following it immediately with a continuation of Tracy's mouth-to-mouth treatment. At his side she still knelt, tense and watchful.

She was beginning to get seriously alarmed

when at last there was a response. Mrs Hamilton sighed deeply and began to breathe again, though she still lay with closed eyes.

'Is she going to be all right?' the niece gasped anxiously, but before anyone could answer there were voices at the door.

Somehow people had sensed that something was wrong, and a middle-aged man in uniform, followed by Colonel Hamilton, pushed his way through.

'Good God!' The Commanding Officer looked down at the ashen-faced woman on the floor and then at the two kneeling beside her. 'What the devil's happened to my wife? Has she fainted?'

'She had a heart attack.' Andrew rose to his feet. 'Luckily there was a nurse here at the time, and she coped.'

'But how did *you* get here, sir? Why was I not sent for?' demanded the other man. They both looked at him blankly and he added impatiently, 'Major Markham, RAMC. I'm in charge of health at the barracks.'

'It was my fault—in a way.' Tracy, who had taken an instant dislike to him, did her best to speak coolly. 'As you've already heard, I was here at the time and I sent Miss—er——' she waved her hand at the niece '—to fetch Mr Lincoln, who is a consultant at the hospital. He was the only medical man at the Ball whom I knew about.'

'Hm, I see.' As way was made for him the Major bent over the patient and felt her pulse.

'Has anyone sent for an ambulance?' Andrew asked quietly.

'I'll do it,' said a voice from the doorway.

They were all standing round in a circle looking down at the prone figure when Mrs Hamilton opened her eyes and spoke in a surprisingly firm voice.

'I'm so very sorry—so stupid——'

Her husband cleared his throat noisily and apparently did not think the apology required a reply. Feeling very sorry for the poor woman, Tracy went down on her knees again and took her hand.

'It could have happened anywhere, any time, Mrs Hamilton. All you have to do now is keep very still and leave us to look after you. Please don't try to talk.'

The Army doctor gave her a sharp look but did not seem able to fault her advice. The Colonel cleared his throat again and said gruffly to Andrew, 'It seems I have to thank you for taking charge, sir. I assure you I'm indeed grateful.'

'Don't thank me. The person you should be grateful to is the nurse, who reacted instantly and started resuscitation. Speed is of the utmost importance in these cases.'

'Er—yes, of course.' The Colonel made Tracy an odd little bow. 'Will someone please tell the band to start playing again? I'm sure my wife would wish the Ball to go on.'

'You'd better make an announcement,' the

doctor pointed out. 'Goodness knows what rumours will be flying round if people aren't told the truth. I suppose you'll want to go in the ambulance?'

'Naturally. My second in command can easily take my place as host.'

It was all done as he had ordered, and Mrs Hamilton was carried out unobtrusively through a back exit, but life had gone out of the party and people began to go home early. Charles, who was not a dancing man, seemed relieved when Tracy suggested they should leave as Nerina would be sure to be lying awake, waiting to be told all about it.

'It seems you've covered yourself with glory, love.' He put his arm round her shoulders and gave her a quick hug. 'Saved the old lady's life, didn't you?'

'Of course not.' She wriggled free. 'It was Andrew Lincoln who got her breathing again.'

'It'll make a good story for Nerina, anyway.' He led the way towards his car.

As Tracy followed him she heard a quiet voice behind her.

'When do you actually leave Gibraltar?'

Her heart was thumping, but she managed to answer calmly, 'Next week.'

Jingling his car keys, Andrew drew level with her. 'How do you feel about it?'

'Oh—er——' she sought frantically for a conventional answer '—I suppose I shall be glad to get down to some real work again. I've had a lazy time here.'

'You prefer the tough jobs?'

'On the whole, yes.' She hesitated, but there was no sign of Angela—no doubt she wished to be picked up at the front door—so there was no reason why she shouldn't prolong this precious moment of conversation. 'Actually, I'm thinking of taking a hospital post for a while. I do that sometimes when I want a real change.'

'It's strange you should say that——' Andrew broke off as Charles started his engine and began backing out of the parking slot.

'Listen——' Andrew detained her momentarily by a light touch on her arm. 'We must meet again before you start packing up. I'll phone you.'

Charles had leaned across and swung open the passenger's door, and Tracy got in, her thoughts a battleground of conflicting emotions. The mere suggestion of a date with Andrew had set her pulses racing, yet she knew perfectly well it would have been more sensible to pretend every minute of her time was fully booked.

She had already said goodbye to him in her heart, so what was the point of further self-torture?

CHAPTER SIX

TRACY sipped her wine and wondered if she was dreaming. If so, it was the loveliest dream she had ever had, and she would like it to go on for ever.

Whoever would have thought when Andrew suggested a date that she would have found herself sharing an intimate dinner at his flat—strictly speaking, his uncle's flat—in Main Street? She had expected another sightseeing drive, though she couldn't imagine what there was left for her to be shown. She had explored every inch of the tiny community, both alone and with Nerina after her friend had ceased to need nursing.

But instead of that he had invited her to dine with him.

'Don't be afraid I shall inflict my own cooking on you,' he said with a laugh. 'I know an excellent freelance cook who's cordon bleu trained, and I shall get her to come in. I can promise you a really first-class meal.'

She would have come if he had offered her bread and cheese, but that was because she was a weak, spineless creature who couldn't resist temptation when it was put in her way. And now that she had admitted all that, she felt she might as well enjoy the occasion and not worry about the pain which must follow it.

The flat was on the upper floor with consulting-rooms below, and was plainly though comfortably furnished, with cream and dark brown as the dominant colours. There were shelves full of books, but no hi-fi equipment or video, and Andrew had made no attempt to stamp his own personality on it.

Outside, the evening was hot and sultry with moisture hanging heavy in the air. The only breeze was provided by Gibraltar's own special wind, the Levanter, which, gathering cloud and mist as it travelled over the sea, did nothing to improve the quality of the atmosphere. Tracy wore a white sun-dress which showed off her tanned shoulders at one end and her bare brown legs at the other. It kept her as cool as she could hope to be, and Andrew looked at her with appreciation and envy.

'Why can't I dress like that?' he asked.

'Because you'd look ridiculous. Besides, your super-cook would think you were in drag!'

He was wearing a short-sleeved grey silk shirt with an open neck and thin tropical trousers, but his dark hair clung to his forehead, and he got up during dinner to increase the speed of the fan.

'If you go back to England when you're planning to, you'll miss the worst of the summer weather,' he said.

'Is it so awful?' Tracy asked lazily, totally relaxed by the delicious food and wine.

'Not awful at all, but it's not the best time of the year—we were having that when you arrived—and sometimes English people don't like the humidity.'

Suddenly Tracy's mind bestirred itself and recalled that he had said 'if'. 'There's no doubt about my going back to England,' she pointed out. 'My flight is booked and I can't imagine anything which would prevent me being on it.'

'Can't you?' Andrew looked at her across the table, holding her gaze, his blue eyes intent. 'Will you be surprised if I tell you I want to undermine that conviction?'

'Undermine it? What on earth do you mean?' Shaken out of her languid mood, she sat up straight and stared at him.

He smiled, but she could see an underlying seriousness. 'I have a proposition to make,' he announced.

'A proposition?' How idiotic she must sound, repeating everything he said! With an attempt at facetiousness, she added, 'That doesn't sound very respectable!'

'I assure you this is a perfectly respectable proposition.' Andrew pushed his plate aside and leaned forward with his arms on the table. 'I'll stop teasing you and plunge right into it. I'm sure you'd prefer that?'

'Of course I would. Do go on!'

'OK, I'm about to do just that. You know, I think, that I'm actually attached to the civilian hospital, though I visit the military one as well. Well, we're desperately short of nurses at the moment. I gather it happens every summer, partly due to holidays, but there's the problem, too, that some of the English nurses find it too hot here in summer and decide to return to England. Anyway, for various reasons, we're short-staffed and about to be more so. Consequently, it would be a godsend if you'd come and spend a few weeks helping out. How about it, Tracy?'

Her head was whirling and she knew she had to choose her words with care. Andrew mustn't be allowed to guess how dynamic had been the effect of his proposition. Working at the hospital she would see him constantly, perhaps even every day if she happened to be attached to his department, but would the resulting pain make it worth it? And surely, when the time eventually came to leave, wouldn't the distress be all the greater?

Much better to leave next week as intended, cut her losses, and find a job that would take up all her energies.

'Well?' he was demanding impatiently.

She mustn't let him see how desperately she wanted to accept. She must tone it down, pretend to consider. . .

'You've taken me completely by surprise. I've never dreamt of such a possibility, but—well, it's strange you should have mentioned it, because I was actually thinking of taking a hospital job next—just for a change.'

'I know—you told me.' He was triumphant, evidently believing it was all settled. 'A hospital job has been dropped right into your lap, without the hassle of packing up and travelling to England, and then getting in touch with your agency and——'

'Hang on!' Tracy held up a hand to stop him. 'You're going much too fast. I haven't agreed to the plan yet.'

He looked momentarily taken aback, but quickly rallied. 'But you will—of course you will! You like Gibraltar and don't really want to leave. Well then, I'm giving you a chance to stay on a bit longer, so why can't you be grateful and say, "Thank you, Andrew, I'd like it very much"?'

'Because I don't like being rushed, or taken for granted either. You must give me time to think.'

'How long do you want? Until the end of this evening?'

'Longer than that! At least until tomorrow.'

How did he imagine she could do any clear thinking while in his presence? Which was a stupid question, if ever there was one, because he didn't know anything about the effect he had on her. At least, she hoped not.

'I can give you until tomorrow lunchtime, but that's all,' he said firmly. 'There'll be quite a bit to arrange. For instance, would you want a room in the nurses' home, or will you remain with Nerina?'

'There's no point in trying to decide that now.'

Tracy's tone was equally firm. 'It must wait until I've made up my mind about the rest of it.'

Andrew smiled. 'Judging by the angle of your chin, I'd better give in gracefully, so let's clear away the supper things and then sit down and talk about something else.'

The cordon bleu lady—who had fully lived up to her proud title—had gone home, and the cleaner who came daily would wash up in the morning. The only thing the host had to do was make coffee, which he accomplished very efficiently. Soon they were seated in armchairs by the window, where a tantalising glimpse of the beautiful garden of the Governor's house nearby gave an illusion of freshness.

'How is your uncle getting on?' Tracy asked.

'He's better than he was but not fit for work.' Andrew sighed. 'I don't really think he'll ever be well enough to come back, poor old chap. It's a shame, because he loved Gibraltar, but I think the best thing for him would be retirement. He's over sixty-five, so there'd be no problem.'

'You seem very fond of him,' she ventured.

'I ought to be—he brought me up, helped by a succession of housekeepers and nannies. My parents were both killed in a motorway crash leaving me nothing but a mortgage—not even brothers and sisters. Even at that early age—I was seven—I made up my mind I would one day have a proper home background like the other kids at school. I didn't realise, of course, that some of the parents weren't all that happy.'

He paused, but Tracy made no comment. After a moment, Andrew continued speaking.

'Uncle David was a bachelor, so I don't suppose he was very pleased at being lumbered with me, though he never let me guess. He got me educated at his own expense and then saw me through medical school. I owe him a lot.'

'No wonder you were willing to break off your own career and come here to look after his job. I've always thought it was very generous of you.'

He shrugged off the praise. 'I suppose I didn't really need to come. They'd have found a locum anyway, but Uncle wanted me to do it. He didn't trust a stranger to look after his patients properly.'

'And now he probably won't come back.' Tracy put down her coffee cup. 'What will you do in that case? Try to get appointed here on a permanent basis, or return to England?'

'That's an easy one! Much as I like Gib, I don't want to work here for ever. I'm aiming for a consultant's post in London or some other big teaching hospital. More coffee?'

When he had poured it he sat down again and gave Tracy one of his penetrating stares. 'That's quite enough about me. Let's talk about you for a change. Do you realise I know hardly anything about you?'

'*I've* got nothing interesting to tell you,' she hedged.

'You can let me be the judge of that.'

His sudden curiosity had caught her unprepared. She rarely talked about her background. Nerina knew only that her parents didn't get on and she was not happy with either of them, and so far she had not even hinted at it to Andrew. Now—perhaps because of the quiet intimacy of the occasion—she felt an urge to talk.

'In a way I've been luckier than you, because I have two parents—at least, some people might think so, but I'm not sure I'd agree with them. When I was small, though, my home seemed all right. It was when I became a teenager that I realised it was far from that.'

Andrew looked puzzled. 'But your parents aren't divorced?'

'No, they're still sharing the same house, but going their separate ways. To my mind it's a terribly unsatisfactory situation, but as they're both totally absorbed in their careers, I suppose they aren't too bothered about it. I think my father probably has the odd affair, but Mum seems able to get along without sex.'

She went on to tell him about her sister's divorce. 'And my brother lives the life of what used to be called "a bachelor gay." You know?'

'I've come across blokes like that.' Andrew was silent for a moment, then went on quietly. 'You still haven't told me anything about *you*. Somehow I get the feeling that all this unhappy background has given you a jaundiced outlook. Am I right?'

'I don't like being called jaundiced,' Tracy protested.

'Isn't it true?'

'Well, yes, perhaps I am—not about life in general, but where marriage is concerned. I'd have to be very sure indeed before I embarked on anything so risky. In fact——' she hesitated '—I'm concentrating on my career for the time being. I might think about getting married when I'm older.'

'That sounds very neat and tidy. What happens if you fall in love?'

Tracy caught her breath and summoned all her resolution to hide from him that he had shot an arrow straight into her heart.

'I've fallen in love a few times,' she said airily, 'but it didn't last. I'm rather inclined to think it very rarely does, and I don't see how anyone can possibly tell at the beginning whether they're going to be one of the lucky ones.'

'Perhaps not, but some people seem to consider it worth risking.'

A moth came blundering in and made for the lamp which Andrew had earlier switched on in the shadowy part of the room. He stood up and pulled down a light cane blind, shutting out Tracy's view of the night sky.

'There's no point in sitting by the window any longer,' he said casually. 'Come over here instead.'

He was standing by the sofa, a big leather-covered one with several cushions. Tracy got up obediently, since to refuse would have been absurd, but she was conscious of increasing tenseness as she crossed the room and sat down.

She was not surprised when Andrew immediately flung himself down very close to her and slid his arm round her shoulders. Resisting the impulse to hold herself rigidly upright, she told herself that almost any man would expect to take advantage of the present circumstances, and managed to relax sufficiently to rest her head against his arm.

But his next question startled her so much that she shot indignantly up again.

'Is there any special man in your life at the moment? Someone in England, for instance?'

'No, there isn't! But for heaven's sake, do I have to submit to this interrogation? What on earth makes you think you've got the right to ask me all these personal questions?'

'Nothing makes me, because I *don't* think it. My only excuse is that I find you intriguing. You're such a bundle of contradictions, like that air of being very much in command of yourself while at the same time having a come-hither look in those innocent grey eyes.'

'Come-hither?' she exploded. 'What a disgusting expression!'

'Sorry, I couldn't think of a better. It expresses my meaning.'

Andrew leaned forward and peered into her face, and she jerked her head aside to avoid his gaze. Her heart was thudding so violently that she felt sure he must be aware of it, and though she tried to struggle when he gently took hold of her chin and turned her back to face him, she found she simply hadn't the strength. He held her for a moment, his finger slowly caressing her cheek but she kept her eyes veiled.

Then he kissed her. And with a long sigh, Tracy allowed her resistance to crumble.

She felt herself lifted up, held for a moment and then put down again, only this time she wasn't sitting upright but lying down full length on the sofa. When Andrew lay down beside her she accepted the dictates of her heart and put both her arms round him and held him close.

How long they remained like that she had no idea. The urgent needs of her body dominated everything, and in particular the passage of time. Yet she was grateful to him because he did not take what she would have so freely given. Instead, with sensuous, intimate caresses, they gave delight to each other without reaching the point of no return.

She had never cared much for one-night stands. To her the act of making love must include at least some feeling of emotion on a higher level than mere passion, and she had no reason to believe Andrew regarded her as anything more than an attractive and—at times—maddening temporary girlfriend.

'How about a drink?' he asked at last, swinging his long legs to the floor and sitting up.

'Only if it's long and cool.'

'I can promise both.'

While he was busy in the kitchen, Tracy found a comb in her bag and tidied her hair. Her make-up was past being revived, but it didn't show up too badly in the lamplight. Sitting far apart, they sipped their drinks and talked trivialities. Tracy had no clue as to Andrew's thoughts, but her own were depressing.

It had been a wonderful evening, and it was over.

'You'll phone me tomorrow and let me know your decision about working at the hospital?' Andrew said as she stood up to leave.

She hesitated, then closed her ears to an inner warning voice. 'I'll tell you now if you like. I've been thinking about it off and on during the evening. I'd like to stay on a bit longer in Gibraltar, so I'll take you up on that offer of a job at the hospital, provided there's not too much red tape.'

'I'm not sure if you need a work permit for staying only a few weeks, but I'll find out. You can leave all that side of it to me.' He opened the outer door and held it for her. 'I suppose they'll want to interview you, but I can fix that too.'

'Thank you.' Tracy went ahead of him down the stairs and exclaimed at the darkness. 'Isn't there a light you can put on?'

'Not until we get to the lobby below. Daft, isn't it? I can't think why my uncle didn't get an electrician to wire up another switch at the top. Excuse me.' He passed her and ran down with the confidence of familiarity.

'Why don't *you* get it done?' she asked. 'It would be a nice surprise for him when—if—he comes back. It really isn't safe for an elderly gentleman to have to negotiate these stairs in semi-darkness.'

The lobby was suddenly flooded with brilliance, and Andrew stood looking up at her.

'It's funny you should say that. Angela made exactly the same suggestion and I half promised to get it done, but—well, I can't convince myself he'll be back, so I've done nothing about it.'

'Angela?'

She hadn't really needed to ask, but it was the only thing she could think of to say.

'Angela Grayson. You met her at the June Ball, didn't you?'

'Oh yes,' Tracy said casually, and was amazed at how natural her voice sounded. 'I do remember her vaguely.'

During the next few days she had plenty of time for regretting that impulsive acceptance of Andrew's suggestion. The very next morning she had wanted to phone him and retract, but pride prevented that. She wasn't in the habit of going back on her word, and after all, it would only be for a short time. Besides, she might not come into contact with Andrew very much.

The interview with an administrator was a mere formality, and Tracy set out on her first morning feeling full of confidence that she would be able to cope—professionally—with whatever lay ahead.

'We're very glad to have you, Nurse Arnold,' Senior Sister Tremayne welcomed her.

She was slim and of uncertain age, with a young face and fair hair turning grey. Keen blue eyes studied the new temporary nurse as she sat opposite, then Sister Tremayne consulted a note on her desk.

'I see you're not going to live in the nurses' home,' she went on. 'Have you got somewhere satisfactory not too far away?'

'The friend whom I came to Gibraltar to nurse would like me to remain with her. I don't really want to, because I'm occupying her only spare room, but I said I'd try it.'

'What about transport?'

'I walked this morning,' said Tracy.

Sister Tremayne's eyebrows shot up. 'My dear girl! We can't have you arriving here feeling like a wet rag. It'll be really hot soon, you know.'

Tracy smiled. 'It was lovely in the early morning today, and going home I can take my time, but if I find it too much it will give me a good excuse for moving into the nurses' home.' She hesitated, then asked diffidently, 'Can you tell me where I'm going to work?'

'I can tell you where I *hope* you'll be working,' Sister told her. 'I'm in charge of the orthopaedic wards and I'd like to keep you with me, but I must warn you that you're likely to be sent anywhere in the hospital at a moment's notice. Quite frankly, Nurse, we don't often get people with your qualifications wanting to work here temporarily, so we intend to make full use of you. I hope you don't mind?'

'Oh, no,' Tracy assured her. 'I'm used to variety in my work as a private nurse, and I like it.'

The less time she spent in the orthopaedic department, the better—in a way.

She was shown round the two wards and told that Mr Lincoln also had a share of the private rooms, then she was handed over to a staff nurse named Rosa Fernandez who undertook to help her settle in.

'How long is it since you've worked in a hospital?' the Gibraltarian girl asked.

She was short, dark and plump, and obviously of Spanish extraction. Tracy fancied she sensed a hint of criticism in her tone, but she had come across it before and took no notice. Hospital nurses always suspected that private nurses were only in it for the money and therefore tended to despise them.

'Quite a while,' Tracy said evasively. 'You'll have to remind me of the routine.'

'It's not very strict here. We're very up-to-date in Gib and the patients are allowed a lot of freedom. Mr Andrew Lincoln is extremely informal. His uncle was quite different—old-fashioned in his manner, but a good surgeon, all the same. We were all sorry when he was taken ill.'

Tracy thought of the conventionally furnished flat, which apparently matched its owner, then shied away from the memory in alarm. She didn't want to be reminded of the place where she had been so insanely happy.

No doubt Angela Grayson had enjoyed her visit too.

She flung herself into the task of learning the patients' names and what was wrong with them, and also where things were kept and all the small items of information which a nurse needed at her fingertips.

It was as she was returning from her coffee break that Senior Sister Tremayne suddenly appeared and summoned her to the office.

'I did warn you, Nurse, that you might be sent somewhere else in the hospital without notice, but I never expected it to happen so quickly. Have you had much theatre experience?'

'Quite a lot,' Tracy said, 'but it was three years ago. My last job at my teaching hospital was as theatre staff nurse.'

'Then you won't have forgotten much, if anything.' Sister sighed and for a moment allowed her own feelings to show. 'I have to tell you there's been a most shocking accident down at the Yacht Club—an explosion on a yacht moored by the jetty—and we've been inundated with casualties so that we have a serious emergency on our hands in theatres. They're not all orthopaedic injuries, of course, but a number of people on yachts nearby were blown on to the quay and sustained fractures of various kinds.'

'That's awful!' Tracy was surprised and shocked. 'I hope nobody was killed?'

'One person, who happened to be in the galley at the time. Fortunately most people were on deck. I take it you have no objection to being seconded to the orthopaedic theatre?'

'None at all. I—I just hope I shall manage to be useful.'

'Don't worry about it. You won't be asked to act as staff nurse, so there shouldn't be any problem. Come with me now and I'll show you the theatre block.'

Her first morning was proving rather more exciting than she had anticipated, Tracy reflected as she followed the senior sister along corridors and up some stairs. By the time they reached the anteroom she was feeling distinctly nervous, but the sight of the familiar layout and figures bustling about clad in green theatre gear soon restored her morale. She would be all right—of course she would!

No one acknowledged her arrival—they were all too busy—so she occupied herself with getting ready. She was scrubbing up at one of the sinks when she heard the arrival of the first patient. As she automatically glanced over her shoulder she saw that two men had followed the trolley in and were deep in low-voiced conversation. One looked as though he might be the anaesthetist and the other was Andrew.

Annoyed because her pulse had quickened even

under those circumstances, Tracy kept her back turned and continued scrubbing. She was just putting on a mask when the door to the theatre opened and a bulky figure looked out.

'Where's the new nurse?'

'Here.' Tracy stepped forward, guessing that this was Theatre Sister.

'You're ready? Good—come and help me in here.'

Andrew was busy with his own preparations and did not turn round. Thankfully, Tracy stepped into the clinical perfection of the operating theatre and hoped she wouldn't draw attention to herself by doing something awful, like dropping an instrument.

'What's the first case?' she asked when she had been given her instructions and stored them carefully in her memory.

'A very tragic one—a boy of twelve who had his leg blown off. Luckily there was someone at hand to control the bleeding, but he needs tidying up—not surprisingly the bone is splintered—and stitching.' Large brown eyes looked sombrely at Tracy over a mask. 'He's English, on holiday with his parents after a prolonged bout of glandular fever.'

'What rotten luck! He'll be suffering badly from shock.'

'Yes, of course. He's already had a transfusion and we've got a good supply of blood ready for emergencies.'

Things were happening. More nurses came in,

and almost immediately the trolley with the unconscious patient on it was wheeled into position so that he could be transferred to the operating table. The stocky dark-eyed anaesthetist was anxiously watching over him, and it was not hard to guess that his condition was causing some concern.

Andrew came in quietly, checked with the anaesthetist and at once began work.

Watching intently, Tracy was totally absorbed in the interest of witnessing an expert at work. She performed her duties without error, much to her relief, but kept as much as possible in the background, grateful that the anonymous green outfit would make it most unlikely that Andrew would be aware of her presence.

In an incredibly short time, the jagged stump was being stitched up neatly and the operation was over. The boy was wheeled away to the recovery-room, and his place was taken by an apparently never-ending line of casualties, some severe, some minor.

They worked all through their lunch break and right up to Tracy's off-duty time. Unaccustomed to standing for such long hours and increasingly conscious of a stomach which had had no attention since a biscuit at coffee time, she felt herself wilting. How awful if she fainted! She had never done such a thing in the theatre, even at her first operation, and she certainly didn't want to disgrace herself now, right in front of Andrew.

Luckily they reached the end without any

WIND OF CHANGE

shame-making collapse, and she followed the others out into the ante-room with a great feeling of relief.

'Thank you all for your help,' Andrew said courteously, glancing round at the nurses who were slowly divesting themselves of masks and gloves, and tossing them into the bin.

He turned round, presenting his back to anyone who felt it her duty to untie the tapes, and Tracy suddenly realised that she was nearest and the others were leaving it to her. So far, since removing her mask, she had managed to keep out of his line of vision. He could hardly see her out of the back of his head, she reasoned, so she stood on tiptoe and, with hands that trembled a little, obeyed his mute request.

Andrew dragged off the shapeless garment, still without turning round. 'Thanks, Tracy,' he said casually over his shoulder.

CHAPTER SEVEN

AFTERWARDS Tracy wondered why on earth she had been so foolish as to imagine Andrew wouldn't notice her, but the fact remained that she had, and therefore to be called by her name was a distinct shock.

'I thought you didn't know I was here,' she said stupidly.

'Of course I knew. Not immediately, of course, but I suddenly sensed that one of my entourage was considerably tensed up and watching my every move with most flattering attention. There was no mistaking those wide grey eyes of yours.'

'Oh, I see.'

'Congratulations on your performance in the theatre,' he went on, dragging off his cap and flinging it into the bin. His thick dark hair stuck to his head in tiny damp curls and he thrust both hands through it, making it stand spikily on end. 'I don't suppose you've done theatre work recently, yet you didn't put a foot wrong—or should I say hand?'

The praise intoxicated her and added to the lightheaded feeling she was already suffering from. 'I enjoyed it, actually, after I stopped being nervous,' she admitted.

Andrew plunged his head into a sink full of cold water, and Tracy, thinking the conversation at an end, moved away to continue restoring her own appearance to normal. But a moment later he accosted her again.

'Are you off duty now?'

She smiled. 'I certainly hope so—I'm starving!'

'That makes two of us. Will there be a meal for you when you get home?'

It had not occurred to Nerina to mention this important matter and Tracy had not liked to say anything about it herself. After all, she could always look in the fridge and find herself something to eat.

'Oh, yes,' she assured him lightly.

'How are you getting back?' was his next question.

'The same way as I got here this morning—on my feet.'

'Don't be daft! You've been on them the whole damn day. I'll give you a lift.' Brushing her automatic protest aside as if she hadn't spoken, he steered her towards the corridor. 'In fact, I'll do better than that. I'll take you to a pub and we'll both have some bar food. How about that?'

Tired and hungry, Tracy nevertheless knew she ought to refuse. Hadn't she set out that morning determined to see as little of Andrew as possible in the future? So where was the sense in letting him take her out for a meal? She knew perfectly well there wasn't any, and it must have been because of the long, hard day that she apparently didn't have the strength to make a stand. Whatever the reason, a short time later she was sitting opposite him at a small table, devouring fish and chips.

'No cordon bleu tonight, I'm afraid,' he apologised.

'This is delicious.' The worst pangs of hunger assuaged, Tracy glanced around. 'This is just like an English pub—horse-brasses and everything.'

'That's one of the nice things about living in Gibraltar. It's different from England in so many ways—especially the climate—and yet it so often feels like home.'

'Will you be sorry to leave?' she asked.

'Not at all,' Andrew said decisively. 'Sometimes I feel I can't wait to get back to London and get on with my career.'

'It means everything to you, doesn't it?' Tracy commented.

'Everything?' He hesitated, clearly debating the matter in his mind. Then he looked straight at her across the table and for a moment held her gaze. 'You may remember that I have another ambition. If I'm to be honest, I have to admit that my career wins by a short head.'

Her eyes dropped to her plate and she did not ask what he meant. She remembered only too well. He wanted to have a happy marriage. And suddenly, without the slightest warning, she lost her temper.

'You want it all, don't you?' she flung at him. 'A

successful career and a perfect home background to make up for not having one when you were little. What makes you think you've got the right to expect all that? Most people have to settle for one or the other, and there's an awful lot who don't get either. Why should *you* be different?'

'Because I'm working on it,' he said mildly.

'You what?'

'I *don't* think I have the right to expect so much, but I see no reason why I shouldn't do my best to achieve it, all the same. And for your further information, I've no patience with couples who want a divorce after a few years of marriage—or even months—because they can't be bothered to try and sort out their problems.'

'It's easy to talk!' Tracy scoffed. 'Maybe if you were a GP instead of an orthopaedist very near the top of the ladder, you'd think differently. You ought to try living in the real world for a change. Things aren't nearly as simple as you seem to imagine.'

As she waited for his reply, she could feel her wrath melting away. It would have been easier to keep up the battle of words if Andrew had lost his temper too, but he remained disgustingly calm. Overwhelmed by weariness, she was about to call a truce when he said something which enraged her all over again.

'Do you remember when I accused you of having a jaundiced outlook?'

'I most certainly do! And I——'

'Denied it indignantly. But I was right, wasn't I, Tracy? You not only see everything through yellow-coloured spectacles but you've got an outsized chip on your shoulder as well.' He shook his head pityingly. 'A very sad case.'

Outraged, she stared furiously at him and, just for a brief moment, thought she discerned a look of amusement. Was it possible he was laughing at her? She had been in deadly earnest, and the idea was intolerable. Unfortunately, her brain seemed to have seized up and she couldn't find the words to refute his accusations.

Controlling her anger, she took refuge in iciness.

'I should be extremely grateful, Andrew, if you'd drive me home. There's no point in continuing this—this discussion.'

'None at all,' he agreed equably, and ushered her politely to the door.

In the morning Tracy toiled up the hill to the hospital wondering what the day had in store for her. It surely couldn't be as awful as the previous one! Even that, though, didn't seem so bad in retrospect, but perhaps that was because she had had a surprisingly good night's sleep.

She had no sooner reported for duty than Senior Sister Tremayne pounced on her.

'I want you to special Matthew Jackson,' she announced, and seeing that Tracy was at a loss, she added, 'The boy who lost his leg.'

'How is he?' asked Tracy.

'Still suffering badly from shock, poor lad. We've put him in a small room by himself and he needs constant monitoring—t.p.r. every hour at present. He's still on a drip, of course, and he's a bit inclined to be restless. You'll need to keep your eye on that.'

'Is he conscious?'

'Oh, yes. But very sleepy because we've been keeping him sedated. He doesn't know about his leg yet. Mr Lincoln doesn't want to tell him until he's a bit stronger, but I don't think it will be possible to wait much longer. The parents will have to be there, naturally, but they both have minor fractures. Matthew's mother was brought along in a wheelchair, but he was asleep, so she only stayed a few minutes.'

Tracy was familiar with the phenomenon of a patient's inability to realise at first that a lower limb was missing. If nobody told Matthew about his terrible disability, he would for a short time go on assuming it was there but heavily bandaged and immobile. In this case there would also be the sedation to confuse his mind.

Staff Nurse Fernandez took her along to the private room where the boy lay. There they found a middle-aged English nurse waiting to be relieved.

'He's anxious about his parents,' she told Tracy in a low voice just outside the door. 'I've explained that they're OK, but he's still muddled and doesn't remember that his mother was here earlier.'

'What's she like? Will she be able to cope?'

The nurse shrugged. 'It's impossible to tell at this stage. Mr Lincoln wants all three of them to be a bit stronger before he breaks the news to Matthew. The parents know, but they need a little time to assimilate anything so terrible.' She glanced over her shoulder at the ashen-faced boy propped up with a cradle over his leg. 'He's all yours now. Have a nice day!'

Tracy thought there was little prospect of that. It was probably going to be restful physically, but mentally it promised to be traumatic.

At first Matthew did not appear to notice the change of nurse, but later, when she was checking his blood-pressure, he opened his eyes wide and stared at her.

'You're different,' he said weakly. 'The other one was old.'

'Hello!' She smiled down at him. 'I've been here nearly an hour, but you were asleep. My name is Tracy, so please call me that instead of Nurse if you like. Are you usually called Matthew, or do you prefer Matt?'

'Matt, please. I don't like Matthew, but I was called after my grandfather.' He frowned and winced as though his head hurt him. 'I can't make out what happened—nobody's told me a thing. Do *you* know?'

Tracy thought it likely he had been told about the explosion, but it had not registered in his confused mind. Now there was intelligence in the hazel eyes and she decided to give him a careful account of the accident.

'I don't know if the explosion was in the galley of your yacht or the one moored next to it,' she finished, 'but a lot of boats were damaged.'

'My father'll never get over it if *Sea Bird* got the worst of it. Mum says he thinks more of his boat than he does of her.' He managed a faint smile.

Tracy smiled back. 'I don't suppose he's the only yachtsman to have had that sort of accusation hurled at him.' She unhooked the chart from the foot of the bed and recorded his blood pressure, glad to note an improvement.

Matt was silent for a while and she thought he had drifted off into a doze, but apparently he had been turning things over in his mind, for he suddenly looked straight at her.

'Tracy——'

'Yes?' She stood up and put her hand on his where it lay on the bedspread. 'Is something the matter?'

'My leg hurts.'

She wanted to ask, 'Which one?' but hated the thought of deliberately deceiving him into believing he still had two. Instead she said quietly, 'What sort of hurt?'

'It's got pains all over it and a sort of dull ache as well. The other one only aches. Come to think of it,' he added thoughtfully, 'I ache all over.'

Tracy's mind raced behind her calm expression,

and she could only hope her perturbation didn't show in her eyes.

'One of your legs—the left one—was quite badly damaged and you're bound to get some pain. You've been written up for painkillers, so would you like something now?'

Matt considered the matter, then refused. 'I don't want anything just yet because the stuff they've been giving me makes me feel so muddled. I keep hoping my parents will come and see me, and I don't want to be half asleep if they do.'

'Your mother was here earlier,' Tracy told him. 'Do you remember?'

'Sort of, but I thought I might have dreamt it—except she was in a wheelchair, wasn't she? I wouldn't have dreamt her like that.' Anxiety suddenly filled his voice. 'She wasn't badly hurt—not as bad as me?'

'Oh, no, I expect she was only in a wheelchair because she was feeling the effects of the explosion.'

'What about my father?'

'I heard he'd got minor fractures, so that probably means a few ribs and an odd bone here and there. I expect he finds it difficult to move just at present.'

The boy seemed relieved. 'I wondered if he'd got a broken leg like me.'

'I don't think so.' Tracy groped frantically for a safer topic of conversation. 'I believe you've had glandular fever. Was it very unpleasant?'

'Not exactly. I mean, it wasn't painful, but it made me so tired. I didn't want to do *anything* at all except lie about and read. The only good thing about it was getting off school. I've missed nearly all this term.'

And likely to miss a great deal more school, Tracy thought pityingly.

They were silent for some time. Matthew appeared half asleep and Tracy picked up a magazine left behind by the previous nurse, and idly turned the pages. Sister Tremayne came in and looked at the chart, then departed again after telling them Mr Lincoln would be round soon.

When she had gone Tracy steeled herself for the meeting. On the way to the hospital she had made up her mind to avoid contact with Andrew as far as was possible while working in his department. She had known there was no hope of that as soon as she was asked to special Matthew. All she could do was keep as much as possible in the background and try not to think about the awful accusations she had hurled at him last evening.

A sound from the corridor jerked her into instant awareness, but it was only an orderly with the drinks trolley.

'I'll have black coffee, please,' Tracy told her. 'What would you like, Matt?'

He chose milky coffee and a biscuit, and Tracy went into the corridor and stood watching as the orderly operated her machinery and produced the drinks.

The woman said something in Spanish which Tracy guessed meant 'I shall have to open a new packet of biscuits', since she had begun to struggle with the polythene wrapping. Eventually, carrying two beakers and, with some difficulty, two biscuits on a cardboard plate, she returned to the room.

The next moment she stood glued to the spot, staring aghast at what her patient had been doing during her brief absence.

The bedspread and sheet hung from the side of the bed, half on the floor, and the cradle was exposed. Beneath it, instead of the leg in plaster which Matt must have been expecting, there was only a bandaged stump.

He was looking at it with a sort of frozen horror. Then his right hand, which had been holding the bedclothes, went limp and the bedding slid to the floor. At the same time his head fell back against the pillows in a merciful faint.

Tracy leapt into life and plunged across the room to the bell. But before she could reach it and ring for help, assistance came from the corridor.

The door had been pushed wide open and Andrew stood there, unattended by sister or staff nurse. With a muffled, 'Good God!' he strode across to join Tracy by the bed and helped her to remove the pillows and lay the patient in the recovery position. That done, he stood motionless for a moment, carefully checking the pulse.

On the other side of the bed Tracy was equally immobile, her eyes on the unconscious boy. She felt sick with guilt and, at the same time, knew it wasn't really her fault. Any nurse specialling a case would consider it safe to step outside into the corridor for a moment with the door partly open behind her. But would anyone else be prepared to admit that? Would Andrew?

She soon found out. Still holding Matthew's wrist, he looked straight at her, and she saw cold fury in his eyes.

'How the hell did this happen?' he demanded in a half whisper.

'I was getting Matt a drink, and he wanted a biscuit too——'

'You were outside? With the door closed?'

'No, of course not. I mean, I was certainly in the corridor, but the door wasn't closed. It—it never entered my head he'd do anything like this.' Automatically she retrieved the bedding from the floor and began to replace it over the cradle.

Andrew frowned and, stealing a glance at him, Tracy saw no softening in his expression.

'What I want to know is—why did he do it? Had you said anything to make him suspicious?'

'No, I hadn't!' She allowed her indignation full rein. 'I'd been very careful, but he kept talking about his leg——'

'Asking questions?'

'Not really. I believed he thought it was broken, and perhaps he did and just wanted to have a look at it.'

'Poor kid—what a ghastly shock for him,

whether he suspected or not.' Andrew looked down compassionately at his patient and then, with a complete change of expression, back at Tracy.

'I still maintain it shouldn't have happened. You know you weren't supposed to leave him alone.'

Tracy gathered her forces to defend herself. 'I don't call what I did leaving him alone. I was only a few yards away for about a minute, and I would have heard if he'd made the slightest sound.'

'But he didn't make a sound, did he? He simply yanked the bedclothes away and saw what had happened. Why weren't they tucked in?'

'Because it was too hot, I suppose. I didn't make his bed——' She broke off as Andrew held up his hand.

'He's coming round.'

The hazel eyes were wide open but still confused. Forgetting her own distress, Tracy smoothed back Matthew's light brown hair with a tender hand, but left it to Andrew to say something.

It was the boy who spoke first. 'What happened—did I faint? I've never fainted in my whole life——'

'You had a shock, old chap,' Andrew told him, his voice very gentle.

'My leg—I uncovered it and it wasn't there! I remember now.' Matthew tried to sit up and fell back with a groan.

'I'll tell you exactly what happened.' Andrew sat

down on the edge of the bed. 'I was going to explain it to you today in any case. Would you like your parents to be here?'

'I want them to come and see me, of course, but I can't wait to be told until they get here. I want to know all about it *now*!'

Andrew spoke to Tracy over his shoulder, his voice still very curt. 'Go and fetch Mr and Mrs Jackson, please, but don't let them think their son is worse.' He smiled at his patient. 'He's actually a great deal stronger and, I believe, quite well enough to be told the truth.'

'Do you want me to tell them anything about what's just taken place?' she asked.

He considered for a moment. 'I think you'd better. It will give them a few minutes to get used to it.'

Tracy was glad to escape and she fled from the room, but as soon as she reached the corridor her steps slowed down. There would be a lot to talk about while she was gone. Andrew would have to explain that the leg was actually blown off, so that there was no hope of saving it, but he would lay the emphasis on the wonderful improvement in artificial legs during recent years, and that Matthew would in future be able to do almost everything with the aid of a new leg.

Mr and Mrs Jackson had been put in a two-bedded side ward so that they could be together, but first she had to find whoever was in charge. It turned out to be Staff Nurse Fernandez, and she felt obliged to give her an account of what had occurred, since she would be bound to hear of it sooner or later.

Although Rosa Fernandez exlaimed in horror, she immediately saw the matter from the nurse's point of view.

'You mustn't blame yourself—it was just one of those things. Anyway, Mr Lincoln was going to break the news this morning, wasn't he? Now the boy's discovered it for himself, and who's to know which would have been less of a shock?'

'Thank you for saying that.' Tracy gave her a wan smile. 'Is Mr Jackson feeling well enough to walk, or will he want a wheelchair too?'

'Neither of them needs one now.' The staff nurse hesitated, then went on, 'Have you met them yet? No? Then I'd better come along and introduce you.'

Mr Jackson was young-looking and had the same pale brown hair as his son. He was having a lot of discomfort with his ribs, and as soon as the two nurses appeared he demanded to know why he had not been strapped up.

'We don't do that now,' Rosa explained, 'but I can assure you the pain will rapidly get less.' Before he could protest further she hastened to introduce Tracy.

Mrs Jackson, a thin-faced young woman with a mass of dark curly hair, burst out eagerly almost before she had finished, 'Is Matt properly conscious now? Can we come and see him?'

'Certainly you can,' said Tracy. 'Mr Lincoln is

with him, and he sent me to fetch you.' She took a deep breath. 'But first I have to explain something.' Speaking quickly but as calmly as possible, she told them what had happened, neither blaming nor excusing herself but simply giving them the facts. When she had reached the end, she looked from one to the other, anxiously assessing their reaction.

They might take the same view as Andrew had done, and be furious because their son had not had their moral support when he found out the truth.

Fortunately it did not seem to occur to them, though they were both staring at her aghast.

Then the father said gruffly, 'The boy had to know some time.'

'How—how did he take it?' Mrs Jackson quavered.

It didn't seem necessary to tell them he had fainted. 'He was deeply shocked, naturally,' Tracy said, 'but that didn't prevent him wanting to be told all the details there and then. He also said, of course, that he wanted to see you both, and Mr Lincoln sent me off to fetch you while he talked to him. Do you both feel strong enough to walk down the corridor? It's not far.'

They assured her that they did, and she led them to their son's private room. Andrew was still sitting on the edge of the bed, but he got up hastily to greet the parents.

'You've been put in the picture?' he asked quietly.

Mrs Jackson made a stifled sound very like a sob,

but her husband answered tautly, 'Yes, thank you—the nurse told us.'

'Then I'll leave the three of you together for a few minutes. We'll be in the corridor if you want us.'

Standing straight and still by the wall, Tracy resisted an impulse to put her hands behind her back. She was no student nurse, hauled up before a senior nursing officer because of some misdemeanour: she was a fully trained and experienced nurse who had done nothing wrong. Pursing her lips slightly, she made no attempt to say anything.

Andrew, too, was silent. He had thrust his hands into his pockets and was frowning out of the window at a gardener who, slowly and lazily, was dead-heading roses. Stealing a glance at his face, Tracy doubted very much whether he actually saw the man.

The murmur of voices coming from the room they had left went on and on. Two nurses deep in conversation came down the corridor, looked curiously from one to the other, and passed on their way. Still neither of them spoke, though Tracy was aware that Andrew was becoming more and more restive.

Eventually he said curtly, 'I'm afraid I lost my temper just now. I'm sorry.'

She supposed she ought to say something casual like, 'That's all right,' but the words stuck in her throat. Last evening, she remembered, she had lost

WIND OF CHANGE

her own temper and he had remained maddeningly calm, but it was impossible to pretend she had not been hurt by his furious condemnation of her conduct.

But he mustn't be allowed to guess at the depth of her distress. She was annoyed about it herself and well aware that she ought to have taken the scolding in her stride.

So she said airily, 'Nurses are always being blamed by doctors for things which aren't their fault. We're all quite used to it, I assure you, and I've already put it out of my mind.'

Surely there was no way he could guess she was lying?

Apparently not, for he said cheerfully, 'That's all right, then. We'll both forget all about it.'

CHAPTER EIGHT

'You look tired,' said Nerina. 'Have you had a strenuous day?'

They were sitting over their after-dinner coffee. Charles had driven into Spain to play polo, and Donna was out with a boyfriend. Upstairs, Jamie slept peacefully.

'I've been helping in Theatres again,' Tracy explained, 'and even though the atmosphere is air-conditioned it always seems more tiring than anywhere else. I suppose it's the standing.' She put down her cup. 'It was only routine cases this time, and it wasn't the orthopaedic theatre either. I've been working with a general surgeon.'

'I expect the word has gone round that you're a useful theatre nurse. More coffee?'

'Please.' She watched it being poured, then went on, 'I don't know about that, and I'm very out of practice, so I have to be extra alert. Perhaps that's why I'm tired.'

'How's that poor boy who lost his leg?' asked Nerina.

'Doing very well. Andrew found him a book about Douglas Bader in his uncle's library—you know, the pilot who lost both legs and refused to let it get him down. He's been reading it avidly ever since and has obviously taken Bader for his hero.'

'I remember seeing the film—ages ago, of course.' Nerina looked uncertainly at her friend and eventually asked diffidently, 'Are you glad you stayed on?'

The question caught Tracy unprepared. She hadn't yet found the answer to it herself.

'I don't know,' she confessed at last. 'Sometimes I think it would have been more sensible to have gone back to England when you stopped needing me.'

'Why *sensible*?'

What on earth had made her phrase it like that? Floundering badly, Tracy snatched at the first excuse which sounded plausible.

'Well, I'm not sure I like Gibraltar as much as I did when I first came. It's not the heat so much as the humidity. That awful Levanter seems to blow every day and——' Running out of words, she let the sentence trail away unfinished.

Nerina's dark eyes studied her doubtfully. 'It blows most of the year, but it's not so noticeable when it's fresher.' She paused, then added quietly, 'I don't think it's the climate that's making you restless. I think there's another reason, but if you don't want to talk about it I shan't try to persuade you.' She waited a moment, but as Tracy said nothing she changed the subject. 'I never told you the real reason why I was so anxious to get home from the hospital.'

'No—no, you didn't.' Tracy nearly added, 'I guessed, though,' but just managed to catch it back in time.

'I don't mind talking about it now it's over.' Nerina took a deep breath. 'It was Donna—I knew she'd fallen for Charles, and I couldn't bear to think of them alone here at night.'

'Didn't you trust him?' Tracy couldn't resist asking.

'Oh, dear——' Nerina sighed, 'it's awful when you put it like that, but it's true that I didn't, not quite. I knew he wouldn't deliberately be unfaithful to me, but I thought he might get carried away if Donna led him on.'

Tracy recalled the night when Jamie had awakened and she had gone to him because Donna seemed to be taking no notice. She'd never really made up her mind about that.

'You seemed much happier after you got home,' she said. 'I suppose that was because you were in the same house and——'

'And I knew you were upstairs and nothing was likely to happen under those circumstances.' Nerina's sober expression changed and she suddenly looked radiant. 'Now, of course, I'm back in my own bed and everything's fine—just fine.'

'I'm so glad,' Tracy told her sincerely. 'I couldn't bear it if your marriage went awry.'

'I hope I wouldn't have let it, but fortunately I never had to face the challenge. Very likely Donna imagined herself in love with Charles, but I would never have let her have my husband—never!'

Tracy hesitated, then said gently, 'But supposing *he* wanted it that way?'

'I'm quite sure he didn't, but it must be difficult for a virile man like Charles not to be tempted when his wife's out of action.'

'I do admire your tolerance, but—well, I can't think why you haven't got rid of Donna,' said Tracy.

'I haven't any real grounds for sacking her, and Jamie loves her dearly. I expect she'll get tired of Gib and want to leave of her own accord before long.'

They sat for a while in silence, each thinking her own thoughts. Tracy was conscious of a great sense of relief. She had been seriously worried about the Maxwell marriage, terrified she might have to add it to her list of matrimonial failures. Now it seemed Nerina didn't believe in failure.

'Andrew would agree with your ideas,' she said suddenly, without stopping to consider the wisdom of such a statement. 'He seems to believe marriages should be *made* to work.'

She had aroused Nerina's interest, that was very clear. Her eyes were alight and her lips slightly parted, as though she were framing a question. It came before Tracy—who had seen the danger—could think of any means of stopping it.

'You've discussed it with him?'

'It cropped up somehow, I forget why. He's very

dogmatic about it and totally ignores all the unhappy marriages littering the place. Personally I seem to trip over them wherever I go.'

'I expect that's because you don't look in the right direction,' Nerina said peaceably.

It was a casual remark, said only to avoid an argument, but it caught Tracy with the force of a blow on the heart. Andrew had accused her of having a jaundiced outlook and she had been angry with him, and now Nerina was saying something similar, though more kindly worded.

Could it possibly be true?

In bed that night she thought about it very seriously, and didn't fall asleep until she had managed to convince herself that both Andrew and Nerina had a completely wrong view of her. She was merely being realistic.

The next day Tracy was back in the orthopaedic wards. Matthew's parents had been moved to a hotel, though they spent a great deal of time at the hospital, and their son had been transferred to the main ward where several other victims of the explosion were still hospitalised. Tracy would have been happy there if it had not been for never knowing when Andrew was likely to appear and do an informal round.

One day he cornered her in the kitchen where she was buttering bread for the patients' tea, as the orderly had gone home with a sick headache caused, so she declared, by the Levanter.

WIND OF CHANGE 141

Lost in thought, her hands working mechanically, Tracy did not hear him come in, but suddenly she felt his scrutiny and whirled round to find him leaning against the wall just inside the door.

'You still haven't forgiven me, have you?' he challenged.

Her hands were trembling, but she managed to say carelessly, 'Forgiven you? I don't know what you're talking about.'

'Of course you do! You're still holding it against me that I lost my temper and accused you of carelessness towards a patient—Matthew. I apologised, didn't I, Tracy? So why do you consider it necessary to find something urgent to do in the sluice, or the office, or the kitchen every time I come into the ward? *Why?*'

'There are things that need to be done in all those places,' she said calmly. 'It's not my fault if they happen to coincide with your visits.'

'Happen be damned! They only occur because you make darned sure they do, so you don't have to come into contact with me.' Andrew folded his arms and glared at her. 'And I'm not leaving this kitchen until you tell me the reason.'

Tracy managed to produce a give-me-patience kind of sigh. 'If you're determined not to believe every word I say, there's not much point in continuing this conversation.' Blindly, she smothered a slice of bread so thick with butter she had to scrape half of it off again.

'To my mind,' he announced, 'there can be only

two possible reasons for your behaviour. One—you're still unforgiving about the telling off I gave you, or two—you no longer wish to continue our—friendship. Which is it?'

Goaded beyond restraint, Tracy rounded on him. 'If you really want to know, it's both reasons. And now will you please go away and leave me in peace?'

The look he gave her was to haunt her for days. There was disbelief in it and reproach, followed by something which looked very like pain, though why he should feel like that Tracy couldn't imagine. There had never been anything serious in their relationship, so why should he object now she had made up her mind to end it?

Wounded vanity, perhaps?

It was a miracle that what remained of the bread got buttered adequately, for Tracy's vision was blurred by tears. Angrily she blinked them away and finished her task. By the time she emerged from the kitchen Andrew had left the ward.

As she walked slowly home that evening, she felt sure she had finally succeeded in her intention to terminate whatever it was which had bound herself and Andrew together during the last few weeks. She ought to be feeling triumphant, but instead of that she was conscious of a heavy weight of sadness. Their blossoming relationship had been very precious to her—*too* precious—and she had deliberately blighted it.

It had taken a lot of courage, so no wonder she felt emotionally drained.

Why had she done it? Why hadn't she let things take their course? Her action had been instinctive rather than reasoned, but she managed to produce an answer of sorts. It was to save worse unhappiness in the future. She already knew that she loved Andrew, whereas he, she felt sure, was only attracted to herself. He would forget her quite quickly after she left Gibraltar and continue his search for the right girl to help him make a happy marriage.

Obviously, the sooner she went away the better, and before long release came more quickly than she had expected.

'There was a phone call for you an hour or so ago,' Charles said a few days later as Tracy arrived home just in time for the evening meal. He paused, then added with unconscious dramatic effect, 'From England.'

For a moment Tracy's heart had leapt, but the mention of England had put paid to the foolish notion that the caller might be Andrew. She was immediately both curious and slightly apprehensive.

'Who was it?' she asked.

'Your father. He wouldn't leave a message except just to ask you to ring him as soon as you came in.'

'I wonder what he can possibly want,' she said half to herself.

Charles turned round from the sideboard with a wine bottle in his hand. 'There's only one way to find out, love, and that's doing what he asked.'

'Ring him back now, Tracy,' Nerina advised, 'otherwise you won't be able to enjoy your meal.'

To receive a call from her father was so unusual that Tracy feared she might not enjoy the meal in any case, but it would certainly be sensible to find out what he wanted as quickly as possible.

She was fortunate in getting through at once, and her father picked up the receiver immediately, as though he had been waiting for the call.

'Hello, Dad!' She tried to sound cheerful and failed utterly. 'Is something wrong?'

Steven Arnold did not waste time in polite enquiries as to her well-being.

'Your mother's ill. She was rushed to hospital yesterday with an emergency appendix. In fact, she came very close to getting—what's it called?'

'Peritonitis?'

'That's it. Seems she'd had this pain off and on for quite a while and was daft enough to think it would go away if she ignored it. The result was it suddenly got urgent.'

'You're quite sure they managed to operate before the abscess burst?' Tracy asked anxiously.

On being reassured she hesitated, not certain whether the peculiarly detached lives led by her parents would include hospital visiting.

'Are you still there?' Steven demanded.

'Yes, of course—I was only thinking. Er—have you got any up-to-date news?'

'I dropped in for a few minutes and she seemed all right to me. She says she'll probably only be in for six or seven days, but she won't be allowed to do much when she comes out, so naturally I thought—we both thought—of you. I know it won't be a glamorous job like you're used to, but I'm sure you won't mind coming home and looking after your own mother for a little while.'

'Of course I won't mind! I'm just thankful it's no worse than an appendicectomy.' Tracy did a quick calculation. 'I'd better move in the day before Mum comes home, so I can get ready for her. Say in three days' time, but I'll ring you again to finalise the arrangements and make sure she's still going on OK.'

'Right. Er—thanks very much.'

He sounded so immensely relieved that she wondered whether he'd thought she might refuse to come. As for her own feelings, she could scarcely have described them. She was concerned, naturally, and very anxious to do what she could to help, but it was no use trying to pretend that having to leave Gibraltar so soon hadn't been a considerable jolt.

Telling herself sternly that, painful or not, it was undoubtedly for the best, Tracy returned to the dining-room to break the news to Nerina and Charles.

They exclaimed in distress because she would so

soon have to leave, but agreed that she had had no choice.

'I hope you're not too worried about your mother to enjoy the last few days?' Charles asked.

Tracy considered the question. She was unlikely to enjoy them anyway, but she didn't want to say so. As for being worried about her mother, an appendicectomy was very much a routine operation these days, and she felt sure there was no cause for undue concern.

'My father didn't think there were any complications,' she said evasively, 'so I don't feel I've got to keep on ringing the hospital for news.'

Gabriella came in with a big dish on which there was beautifully arranged a whole salmon in aspic decorated with colourful salad. Tracy looked at it admiringly and thought how much she was going to miss the lovely food she had had in Gibraltar.

Concentrate on the ordinary everyday things, she told herself fiercely. Don't think about the people.

Nerina was talking about the local hospital. 'Will they let you leave immediately under the circumstances?'

'Perhaps, but I shan't ask them. I think it's only fair to work at least another couple of days. I'll keep just one day for packing and—er—anything else that crops up.'

They began to make suggestions as to how she should spend her last day. Tracy let them get on with it and said very little. At that moment she had no idea what she intended to do—or why something deep down inside her was urging her to keep the day free.

When they were leaving the table Nerina came to put her arm round Tracy's shoulders. 'We're going to miss you terribly!' she exclaimed emotionally.

Tracy forced a smile. 'I should think you'll be glad to get rid of me. It was early spring when I came, and now it's full summer.'

'And I was flat on my back and now I'm very nearly fully recovered. All due to your nursing.'

'That's a load of rubbish——' Tracy broke off as Charles interrupted.

'I'll leave you two girls to have a heart-to-heart and take myself off to the Mess for a couple of hours. See you!'

Unwisely, Tracy completed what she had been going to say. 'It was Andrew who insisted on leaving your back to heal itself, instead of performing a difficult and dangerous operation.'

'All right, he can have some of the credit.' Nerina sat down on the sofa and picked up some knitting. She glanced across at her friend, hesitated, then added, 'You two don't seem to see so much of each other now. At one time I thought——'

Tracy bit her lip in vexation. By mentioning Andrew she had laid herself wide open to some of Nerina's gentle probing.

'You thought we were having an affair?'

'Well, actually I was thinking on quite different

lines. I rather hoped your friendship might lead to something more serious.'

'Unfortunately for your matchmaking, Andrew and I view marriage rather differently. I assure you, it wouldn't have worked. Not that we ever considered it,' Tracy added hastily.

'I do hope you'll get married some day,' said Nerina earnestly. 'I can really recommend it; in spite of ups and downs it's far better than being single.'

Tracy laughed. 'You're incurably romantic and I hope you stay that way, but marriage is not for me. Not yet, anyway.'

There was a brief silence while Nerina consulted her pattern. When she had checked the stitches, she said diffidently, 'I suppose you fancy yourself as the modern equivalent of a hospital matron? You'd have to leave private nursing and take a hospital job as a sister, but if your ambitions lie in that direction——'

'They don't at present, thank you, and I'm pretty sure they never will. I'm enjoying my chosen form of nursing, and when I've seen Mum through this little hiccup in her career I shall look out for a really tough job.' And forget all about Andrew, Tracy added silently to herself.

'Like mother, like daughter,' Nerina said lightly.

The comment hit Tracy like a physical blow. It wasn't true, was it? Surely she didn't in the least resemble that apparently cold, self-contained woman who had turned her back on her marriage and was devoting herself to teaching English to other people's childen? She was quite prepared to admit it was largely her parents' loveless marriage which had made her afraid to risk anything similar, but that didn't mean she was like her mother.

She might get like her, though.

'I'm sorry you're leaving us so soon, Nurse Arnold,' Senior Sister Tremayne said regretfully, 'but I quite understand the reason. Perhaps you might consider returning to Gibraltar when you've finished looking after your mother? We should be glad to offer you a permanent post at the hospital if you're interested.' She turned to Andrew, who had been listening to the conversation with downbent head. 'Don't you agree, Mr Lincoln?'

His expression was deadpan, his voice detached. 'It's not for me to say, Sister, since I shall shortly be leaving myself, but I've rather got the impression that Nurse Arnold would like to resume her private nursing as soon as possible.'

Tracy spoke quickly, before the sister could comment. 'I only expected to be away from England about three weeks, and I've stayed much longer than that. For various reasons I'd like to get back.'

'In that case——' Sister's tone was unusually acid '—I fail to understand why you applied to the hospital for a temporary post which was likely to last throughout the summer.'

Tracy failed to understand it too.

Excusing herself, she left the office and returned

to the ward. It had been a blow to discover Andrew there when she sought out Sister Tremayne to break the news to her. Perhaps, in view of the way news always travelled along the hospital grapevine, she had been absurdly optimistic to hope she might slip away without his becoming aware of her intention. The fact remained that she *had* thought it possible.

Even now, she still hoped she might manage to escape without talking to him anywhere except in the hospital. Consequently it was all the more extraordinary that she should find herself agreeing to spend the whole of her last day with him.

It was arranged over the telephone, and at first she flatly refused to even comtemplate the outing. 'I've got a lot of packing,' she protested. 'It's amazing how much you accumulate when you're away from home for quite a while.'

'Unless you're a great deal less efficient than I believe, it won't take you all day. We can easily arrange to be back in the early evening, which gives you plenty of time.' His voice changed and became impatient. 'Quit stalling, Tracy. You can't possibly leave without a trip to North Africa among your experiences.'

'North Africa?' she echoed faintly.

'Morocco, to be exact. In other words, Tangier. We'll catch the hovercraft early in the morning and that will give us almost a whole day there.'

'How long does the crossing take?'

'Under the hour, or we could go by air. That would be quicker.'

'No. I'd rather cross the Strait by sea——'

'You'll come, then?' He was triumphant.

'I haven't said so,' she protested.

'But you're pretty near it.' Andrew's tone changed again. 'Please, Tracy, don't say no. You'll always regret it if you don't visit Tangier while you've got the chance. It's quite different from Gibraltar, you know, and a marvellous place to buy presents to take home.'

Except for her mother, she hadn't anyone to take a present to, but she did not mention that. Since she was obviously going to give in and agree to the arrangement, it was important he should believe it was only for sightseeing and souvenir-buying.

'OK then,' she said abruptly. 'Since you're so pressing I'll let you show me Tangier. What time do we start?'

'I'll call for you at half-eight. Mind you're ready.'

There was a sharp click and the line went dead. Tracy replaced her own receiver more slowly, then almost immediately stretched out her hand to pick it up again. She must be crazy, agreeing to an excursion with Andrew which would take up all her last day! What would Nerina think?

Andrew had been phoning from his consulting-rooms and she didn't know the number. Reluctantly she picked up the book, then hesitated again. Perhaps if she explained to Nerina. . .

Explained what? That she so desperately wanted

to spend a few more hours in Andrew's company that she was prepared to ditch her best friend? Put like that it sounded awful, nevertheless Tracy went in search of Nerina, whom she found upstairs putting Jamie to bed, since it was Donna's day off.

'You've come just at the right moment,' Nerina greeted her. 'Would you mind lifting Jamie out of the bath for me? I'm still being careful with my back.'

'I'm glad to hear it.' Tracy scooped up the protesting little boy and dumped him on his mother's lap, getting considerably wet in the process. She waited until his indignant yells had subsided, then broached the subject uppermost in her mind. 'I'm feeling very guilty,' she announced.

'Really?' Nerina did not sound very impressed. 'So what crime have you committed, then?'

Tracy took a deep breath and plunged. 'Andrew rang me up and invited me to go with him to Tangier the day before I leave. I was tempted because I haven't been able to fit it in in spite of being here so long, and I'm afraid I accepted without giving it proper thought. Then, of course, it occurred to me that you might be planning something.'

There was a slight pause, then Nerina said carefully, 'I expect you'd like to visit Tangier, wouldn't you?'

'Well, as I said, I've always meant to but——'

'It would be a pity to return to England without seeing a Moorish town when there's one so near.

I'm sure you'd enjoy it, so please don't worry about going off with Andrew. I don't mind— honestly.'

'You're sure?' Tracy persisted.

'Of course I'm sure! Bring Andrew back to dinner if you like and we'll have a special celebration meal.'

Tracy smiled. 'Because I'm leaving?'

'That wasn't the celebration I had in mind,' Nerina told her nonchalantly.

CHAPTER NINE

HER VERY last day. Tracy awoke with that thought in her mind and for a moment she was on the verge of tears. Angrily, she blinked them away and took herself sternly to task. It was going to be a wonderful day, a particularly bright jewel in life's necklace of precious memories, so what had she got to be unhappy about?

By the time Andrew called for her she was apparently on top of the world. He too seemed in good spirits, and they boarded the hovercraft in an aura of good fellowship.

Seen from the sea, Tangier looked large and rather grand, with big, yellowish-cream houses climbing up and down small hills, numerous mosques holding their minarets proudly aloft and, nearer the coastline, tall tower blocks of hotels. As they drew nearer, they saw gardens blazing with flowers, a great many palm trees, and stretches of parched grass baking under a fierce blue sky. But by the time they actually set foot in Morocco, the whole aspect of the town had completely changed.

Tall, grey, crumbling houses crowded together near the waterfront, the black mouths of alleys yawning between their lower floors. A slow-moving crowd of people drifted along—tourists in gay summer clothing, Moslem women clad in black from head to foot, their eyes gazing mysteriously over their yashmaks, and men in every variation of dress from Western to Eastern.

'We'll get a taxi and go for a ride around first,' Andrew said. 'And after that I expect you'd like to explore on foot.'

'It doesn't look as though there's much room for motor traffic,' Tracy commented.

'It's only possible along the main streets. In this rabbit-warren you either have to ride a donkey or walk.'

Tracy glanced at uneven steps and steep cobbled slopes winding away into the labyrinth. 'Are Westerners really safe in there? It looks horribly sinister from here.'

'You'll be safe enough with me.' Andrew slipped his arm into hers. 'But I wouldn't advise going by yourself.'

'I'm not likely to do that! I'd be petrified.'

They found a taxi without much difficulty and drove along a wide, tree-lined street with Western shops on both sides. Sitting close together in the middle of the back seat, their bodies touching from shoulder to calf and hands linked, they continued to play their role of tourists and talked about only what they could see from the windows.

Tracy tried to make intelligent comments and ask the right questions, but it seemed to her she was functioning on two different levels, one very much on the surface and the other deep down close to her heart. Every now and then her true feelings would threaten to rise to the top and spoil the game of 'let's pretend', but she quelled them sternly and they retreated again.

By the time their driver had shown them everything he considered they should see, it was lunchtime, and he dropped them outside a restaurant serving Moroccan food, hot and spicy but nevertheless delicious. They washed it down with mint tea and finished the meal with tiny cakes filled with a delectable almond filling.

'Now for the souks,' said Andrew.

'What exactly *are* they?'

'The native version of a shopping centre.' He steered her across the road, dodging bicycles and an overladen donkey. 'Incidentally, Tracy, if you want to buy anything you mustn't even think about paying what you're asked. Bargaining is part of their lives, and they enjoy it.'

'It isn't part of mine,' she said stubbornly, 'and I certainly wouldn't be any good at it. I don't expect I shall buy anything.'

Andrew smiled. 'Wait until you see the incredibly low prices.'

'If they're so low, I don't think that tourists ought to try and knock some more off. After all, these people live very near the poverty line, don't they?'

'Lots of them are well below it, but they really do enjoy their bargaining. They'd take a pretty poor view of you if you paid the first price mentioned.'

They had reached an ancient archway with a steady flow of holidaymakers pouring through it, and Tracy assumed it was the entrance to the 'shopping centre'. Set on continuing the argument, she at first scarcely noticed the goods offered for sale.

'We didn't change any money, so I don't see it's possible to do any shopping,' she said. 'I don't even know the name of the local currency.'

'Dirhams, but it doesn't matter you haven't got any. All the traders will expect you to give them English money, and they speak English too, so there's no problem.'

Andrew had turned into a courier again, and as they strolled along the uneven dirty street, only a few yards wide, Tracy was overwhelmed by a wave of despondency. It wasn't a guide book she wanted but a warm, living man who loved her the way she loved him. More than ever she felt certain it had been crazy to give up this last day to hours of torture instead of spending it peaceably with Nerina.

With an effort she shelved her unhappy thoughts and gave her attention to the tiny shops, which were little more than a shelf in an open window. She could see nothing which attracted her in the slightest, but it was different when Andrew took her into a carpet emporium.

Exquisite, intricately patterned rugs of all sizes

were flipped over for their inspection. The colours were subtle and yet brilliant, the materials used had a silky sheen.

'I'd certainly fall for one of those if I had anywhere to put it.' Tracy gazed entranced at the wonderful display. 'One of the disadvantages of private nursing is that you don't have a home of your own.'

'I'm going to buy one, though I haven't anywhere either at the moment. I hope soon to have a flat in London, and the rug will be a reminder of——' Andrew hesitated, searching for the right words.

'Of what?' Tracy asked, then wished she hadn't, but Andrew's answer was quite undisturbing.

'Of our visit to Tangier,' he finished calmly.

They left the carpet showroom and began a slow descent towards the waterfront. It was very crowded now and at times they had to walk one behind the other. As they moved slowly along, keeping pace with the crowd, they were besieged by street salesmen with beautiful embroidered kaftans apparently made of silk. Draped carelessly over one not-too-clean arm, they were waved tantalisingly in front of the Western women.

'I absolutely *must* have one of those!' Tracy exclaimed, forgetting all her previous protestations. 'Will you bargain for one for me?'

'Better than that—I'll buy you one as a present.'

'No, please—I don't want you to do that.'

'Why not?' demanded Andrew, stopping and

looking down into her eyes with one of his soul-searching stares.

Apart from an instinctive independence—which he wouldn't have approved of—Tracy could think of no reason. In fact, she now found she very much wanted him to buy her a present. Like the rug, it would be a reminder of Tangier.

If only the two Moroccan souvenirs—the rug and the kaftan—were to share the same future!

She mustn't let herself think like that. Getting a firm grip on her emotions, Tracy said humbly, 'Please, Andrew, I'd very much like you to buy me a kaftan.'

He looked at her in surprise, grinned but made no comment. When they were accosted by the next salesman she chose a white one embroidered in silver and gold.

'Twenty pounds,' said the man, eventually accepting a fiver.

After that they bought several items, and Tracy even managed to bargain for a camel beautifully crafted of leather with a fierce-looking Bedouin astride.

'We must save enough time for a proper look at the Medina,' said Andrew.

'What's that?'

'The street where craftsmen sit in their shops working at whatever they sell. It's very interesting.'

'I expect it is,' she agreed meekly.

But Tracy was destined not to explore the Medina after all.

It happened a few minutes after they had been photographed by a tall dark-skinned young man with an instant camera. Andrew ignored him and walked on among the press of people, but Tracy felt a sudden need to possess the picture. Calling out to him to wait, she searched her handbag for the one pound the photographer was asking.

She had just located the coin—her last—and received the snap in exchange when a crowd of teenage boys in native dress burst out of a side turning and pushed rudely between Tracy and the cameraman.

She reeled back, only just avoiding losing her footing, and instinctively tightened her grip on her bag. Unfortunately it was open, since she had only just stowed the snap in a pocket, and her instinctive reaction was to check the contents before closing it. Not intending to do much shopping, she had not brought her wallet and nearly all her cash had been spent, which was fortunate, because her purse had vanished.

So had Andrew.

He had been only just in front of her when she stopped to pay for the photograph and she remembered calling out to him to wait. After that her attention was given to the photograher, and she hadn't realised Andrew had apparently not heard her.

He would miss her almost immediately—she was sure of that—and would turn back, but there was no sense in standing still and waiting for him to reappear. Choosing the alley down which she was certain he had disappeared, since most of the tourists seemed to be going in that direction, Tracy set off in pursuit.

It ought to be quite easy to see his head above the crowd, but somehow she couldn't. The lane was steep and she had a good view of the bobbing heads in front of her, but there was no thick thatch of dark hair among them. Quickening her pace, Tracy squeezed past a group of holidaymakers and was soon at the bottom of the hill.

Still no sign of Andrew.

Aware of the beginning of panic and fighting it off, she halted on a corner where several alleys met. It was impossible to decide which one to take, and she came to the conclusion that it would be better to stay where she was and let him find her.

It turned out to be an unwise decision. Seeing a foreign girl standing alone and provocatively dressed, the local youths evidently considered her fair game. They began to hover round her, making remarks in their own language and roaring with laughter. Tracy could feel her cheeks growing hot, but somehow she managed to keep her dignity, though her heart had begun to beat uncomfortably fast. Standing rigidly on her corner, she ignored them as best she could and prayed that Andrew would soon turn up.

If only she wasn't wearing a sundress. . .Compared with the way their own women dressed, it must look outrageously sexy.

She stole a peep at her watch, fearing it might be snatched from her wrist if her tormentors got a look at it. It seemed incredible that less than ten minutes had gone by since she had stopped to buy the photograph and Andrew vanished. Trying to think sensibly, she decided to endure her present situation for five more minutes and then make her way slowly towards the hovercraft terminal. She had no money and Andrew had her ticket, so she didn't try to plan any further than that.

The youths were growing bolder. They drew nearer, their bodies exuding a powerful odour of strong scent mingled with sweat. Coffee-coloured fingers actually touched her bare skin, lingering to caress, and she couldn't repress a shudder. She tried to step backwards, only to find herself in close contact with someone who had squeezed in behind her.

She was really frightened now. If they decided to drag her off to some secret lair, she would be powerless to resist, and it seemed unlikely anyone would come to her rescue. The passers-by had mostly not even noticed her predicament, though one or two had glanced at her askance and hurried past, probably imagining she had asked for what she was getting.

Just as she felt she couldn't bear it another minute, her tormentors suddenly reeled back and began to slink away. A tall dark man with blazing blue eyes had swept them aside by sheer force of his personality, or so it seemed, since he had done nothing more intimidating than push his way to her side.

'Andrew! Oh, Andrew——' Tracy was almost sobbing in her relief. She sprang forward and would have thrown her arms round him if he had not held her off.

'For God's sake, be careful!' he snapped. 'We don't want any more trouble.'

'Wh-what do you mean?' She gazed up at him in alarm.

'Surely you know people don't embrace each other in the street in Moslem countries? You don't want to be flung into prison, do you?'

He was exaggerating, Tracy felt sure, but she obediently let her arms drop to her sides and summoned what shreds of dignity remained to her. Bewildered and hurt, she suddenly remembered that attack was supposed to be the best form of defence.

'What on earth happened to you?' she demanded. 'I was terribly scared when I found you'd disappeared!'

'Do you imagine I wasn't worried? One moment you were there, close behind me, and then a few seconds later you'd completely vanished.'

'I stopped to buy that photograph—I called out to you——'

'I didn't hear you.'

'Then some boys pushed between the photographer and me and one of them must have snatched my purse. Luckily it was nearly empty. When I'd got over the shock of that I looked for you and couldn't see you anywhere.'

'Then why the hell didn't you stay where you were?' Andrew demanded. 'I would soon have found you.'

Tracy tilted her chin. 'Because *I* thought I'd soon catch you up if I followed the crowd down the hill, but I didn't see any sign of you, and I got worried and decided to stand still and let you find me.'

'Standing alone on a street corner really was asking for trouble,' Andrew said grimly.

'I didn't know that, did I?' Tracy was getting over her fright and her indignation was growing. 'Anyway, where did you get to? You must have left the mainstream of tourists or I would have caught up with you.'

Andrew looked at his watch. 'We'd better sort this out on our way to the docks.'

They began to walk along the Medina, passing fascinating craft workshops and beautiful displays of exotic fruits and vegetables without a second glance.

'To begin with,' Andrew went on, 'it never occurred to me you'd want to buy that photograph. I took it for granted it would be terrible. Was it?'

Tracy suddenly realised she hadn't even glanced at the cause of all this trouble, and she pulled it out of her bag. The two faces stared back at her, laughing and happy, and a sob welled up inside her and threatened to develop. If a photographer were to snap them now, how different they would look.

'It's—it's quite good,' she faltered.

'So it is.' Andrew took it from her and studied it. 'Another souvenir,' he added, handing it back.

She put it away carefully and pulled herself together. 'Go on. I'm still waiting to hear how you managed to disappear.'

'It was quite simple. You remember there were several alleys branching off? Well, at the same moment as you stopped—though I didn't know you had—I saw a woman slip on the cobbles in one of them. She was overweight and wearing ridiculous high heels, and she fell heavily. Her friend tried to heave her up, and naturally I went to help, assuming you'd seen the fall too and would be behind me.

'We managed to get her into a doorway, but there was nowhere to sit and I had to hang on for a minute to make sure she wasn't going to pass out.'

'When did you realise I wasn't there?' Tracy asked.

'Just about then, I suppose.'

'You took your time over it,' she told him.

Andrew immediately reacted indignantly. 'I had plenty to think about. At first I didn't know whether she was hurt. She could easily have sprained her ankle, or even broken it, in those daft shoes, and my mind was busy with what I was going to do if she proved to be incapable of walking. Luckily she hadn't done any real damage and I got away as soon as I could, and started looking for you.'

'Was she English?' asked Tracy.

'Yes, fortunately.' He paused, then asked, 'Well? Are you satisfied I didn't deliberately abandon you?'

Tracy knew she ought to assure him that she was, and perhaps apologise for her accusation, but somehow the words wouldn't come, and she merely mumbled that she supposed so.

There was a strained silence, then Andrew said abruptly, 'I'm sorry all this happened, but I hope you won't let it spoil your memories of the day.'

At that moment Tracy felt the day was ruined. She suspected it was silly of her, that she would get over her fright and remember only the wonderful part which preceded it, but it was impossible for her to say so, to explain that it wasn't the unfortunate incident in the souk which was distressing her now. It was because they had quarrelled over it.

Andrew was waiting for an answer. Making a great effort, she told him with an entirely false cheerfulness that it had been a super day and she would do her utmost to forget the last part of it.

The hovercraft was waiting and they found good seats, but as far as Tracy was concerned the other passengers made so little impact on her that they might just as well have been ghosts. The only person who had any reality was the man sitting close beside her, his fingers entwined with hers. She was conscious of him in every fibre of her being, and the longing for a more intimate contact was almost unbearable.

'Is Charles driving you to the airport?' he asked suddenly.

'He says so.'

After that brief exchange they resumed their silence. As the Rock grew steadily larger and more dramatic, Tracy watched it sadly. So much had happened to her during the weeks she had spent there. She had explored a new place and she had had a new experience. She had fallen in love, and this time she knew it was for real. This time she would not get over it without a great deal of anguish. Perhaps not ever.

When they were driving from the docks she made a great effort to return to normal and remember her manners.

'I can't thank you enough for taking me, Andrew. I've thoroughly enjoyed it.'

'It was my pleasure,' he said formally. 'Er—I'm really sorry you had that unfortunate experience when we lost each other and I'm afraid I wasn't as sympathetic as I should have been. I hope you'll believe me when I assure you it was because I'd been so worried.'

'I understand.' She hurried to change the subject. 'I think Nerina's expecting you back to supper.'

Holding her breath, she waited for his reply,

torn between a yearning to keep him with her a little longer and the certain knowledge that to say goodbye now in broad daylight, with both of them behaving like casual friends, would make a cleaner break than to wait until after supper.

Andrew couldn't possibly be facing the same problem, yet he was taking a long time to answer.

'I don't think I will, thanks,' he said eventually. 'I want to put through a call to England to see if I can get some up-to-date information about my uncle. I had rather a worrying letter from him yesterday in which he seemed very confused, and when I rang last evening I couldn't get hold of his doctor. I'd like to try again tonight.'

'And you haven't said a word about it all day!' Tracy exclaimed. 'It must have been there, at the back of your mind, all the time.'

'Er—no, I'm afraid it wasn't—only now and then. After all, there was nothing I could do about it in Tangier, and I had plenty of other things to think about.'

'Like me getting lost——' Tracy broke off and apologised. 'Sorry, I didn't mean to bring that up again.' Noticing that the car was slowing down, she looked out of the window. 'Oh, dear, we're nearly there.'

Andrew must have noticed her involuntary exclamation, but he gave no sign. He brought the car gently to a halt, then stretched out his left hand and laid it on hers. 'I'm not going to say goodbye, because I'm sure we shall meet again—some time, somewhere.'

'You must be thinking of that old wartime song "We'll meet again".' Tracy's voice was shaking. 'I can't believe it will happen to us.'

'Why not? Medical people are always meeting each other.'

'In hospitals—yes. But I'm a private nurse.'

His grip tightened. She could feel him looking at her, but she did not dare to turn her head and meet his eyes.

'Did I ever remark on what an argumentative girl you are?' he asked.

'Only about a dozen times!'

Her laugh was very close to tears and somehow she managed to wriggle her hand free. But before she could open the door Andrew's arms came round her and she was held in a vice-like grip, and she couldn't have escaped if she had wanted to. Which she didn't.

He kissed her fiercely, forcing her mouth open and bruising her lips, and the pain was a delight to her and she longed for more. She pressed both hands on the back of his head, feeling the dark springing hair between her fingers, and drew him closer still. It seemed to her then that she was drowning in a sea of emotion which was so deep and vast she didn't think she would ever surface again.

Gradually the simple need for air obliged them to relax their desperate grip of each other. Hearts thudding, they drew slightly apart, and over Andrew's shoulder Tracy became aware of the interested stare of a passing soldier.

He was the first to speak, his voice strangely hoarse. 'I shall miss you, Tracy love. Nobody to quarrel with—what on earth shall I do?'

Tracy never knew what made her answer as she did. The words popped into her mind and were said before she could stop them.

'What about Angela? Or doesn't she argue with you?'

'Angela? I don't understand.' He sounded genuinely bewildered.

'She's a friend of yours, isn't she?'

'She's married,' Andrew said curtly.

'So?'

'So I'm not in the habit of dating married women.'

'She came to your flat——' she began.

'To return a book I'd lent her husband. Knowing her reputation—and because it was late—I got her out of it as fast as I could and congratulated myself on a lucky escape.' He paused, then went relentlessly on. 'And if you'd like to know why I partnered her at the June Ball, it was because she asked me very nicely and I didn't know so much about her then. Does that satisfy you?'

Tracy couldn't speak. They were going to part fighting and it was all her fault, and she couldn't bear it. Blindly she put out her hand and groped for the door handle.

'Thank you again.' She was out of the car and once more in possession of a voice, even though it didn't sound much like her normal one. 'I shall always remember this lovely day.' Taking a deep breath, she finished with a rush. 'Goodbye, Andrew. I hope you get better news of your uncle.'

And with her head held high and a breaking heart, she walked up the garden path, away from him.

CHAPTER TEN

TRACY'S Metro stood outside her parents' house, exactly as she had left it. That it was unvandalised was due to the fact that they lived in a quiet cul-de-sac. On this particular morning the dusty paintwork was bespattered with the raindrops which had fallen earlier, a depressing greeting for Tracy when she got off the plane at Gatwick.

Although it was summer and the gardens were full of flowers, all the colours seemed muted after the brilliance of Gibraltar. The rain-washed blue of the sky was slightly misty and the sun less bright; only the grass was greener. Normally she would have said she preferred the softness of her own country to the vividness of the Mediterranean, but not in her present mood.

The house was empty, airless and far too tidy. Her mother's cleaning lady had done her job well and erased almost every sign of human occupancy. Except for a slight shabbiness, it could have been a show house on some new estate. Even Tracy's bedroom was unnaturally neat, and in a flurry of impatience she began to unpack, deliberately strewing her possessions on chair and bed and floor.

Her souvenirs made her pause, particularly her

favourite—the leather camel—and she held it in her hand, gazing into the rider's small fierce eyes and remembering the circumstances under which it had been bought. He looked as exotic as his mount and considerably less tamed. If he wanted something he would go all out for it and not rest until he was in triumphant possession.

Why couldn't she have been like that?

Last of all she studied the photograph. The two laughing faces stared back at her, and she wondered if they could possibly have been as happy as they looked. If so, it had been their last moment of pleasure in each other's company, for immediately afterwards they had been separated, and later on Andrew had been angry and she indignant. And after that there had been nothing left but to say goodbye.

If she had behaved differently, shown more of her gentler side instead of hiding her feelings for fear of getting hurt, she could probably have had an affair with Andrew.

It would have been *something* to remember.

Tracy sighed, then made an effort to pull herself together. When she had put everything away she turned her attention to the planning of meals. She had just returned from a brief shopping expedition when her mother phoned from the hospital to confirm that she would be discharged in the morning.

'I was intending to visit you this evening,' Tracy said.

'It hardly seems worthwhile,' Joan Arnold told her briskly. 'You'll be tired after your journey.'

'OK, then. How are you feeling?'

'I find moving about rather painful and my legs are ridiculously wobbly, but otherwise I'm fine. I don't think I shall need you to look after me for very long.'

'I shall definitely stay for two weeks,' Tracy said firmly, 'and then we'll review the situation.'

They were the longest two weeks of her nursing career. Her father she scarcely saw at all, though he slept at home, and her mother was bored and restless. She was making a wonderful recovery and aching to be back at school, but the doctor was insisting on a month at home.

'It's no good going back until you can drive again,' Tracy pointed out, 'and that won't be until at least the third week.'

The day her mother tried out her car, she rang up the agency and asked to be given a really tough job.

'I can't promise you one right away,' said the ex-Nursing Officer who ran it. 'Or are you prepared to wait for one?'

Tracy hesitated. 'I'll wait a little while,' she temporised. 'Will it be all right if I give you a ring when I'm getting desperate?'

The woman laughed. 'You do that, but I hope it won't be necessary.'

Time passed slowly and both mother and daughter did a great deal of reading, though Tracy's mind was not always on the print which passed before her eyes. Joan preferred newspapers, and generally managed to spend most of the morning deep in the *Daily Telegraph*.

'What was the name of Nerina's doctor?' she asked suddenly, startling Tracy so much that for a moment she was speechless.

Hastily she pulled herself together. 'Lincoln, but why——'

'I've just been reading an obituary—one of the short ones down at the bottom of the page—and apparently he's just died.'

'D-died?' Tracy's voice sounded as though someone was trying to strangle her, and the whole room tilted sickeningly.

Joan noticed nothing. 'That's what I said. He seems to have been quite a famous orthopaedist before he moved to Gibraltar—got the MBE——'

Such a wave of relief washed over Tracy that she felt sick. She had been a fool not to have guessed right at the beginning that it was Andrew's uncle her mother was talking about, but the sudden mention of the name Lincoln had turned her brain upside down. Speaking as calmly as she could, she hurried to put matters right.

Andrew would be upset. His affection and gratitude towards the old man had been deeply felt. He would now have to decide whether to stay on in Gibraltar—which seemed most unlikely—or go all out for the sort of post he really wanted in London or some other big city.

In the meantime he would have to come to England for the funeral.

As soon as her mother had disappeared upstairs for the afternoon nap she still felt a need for, Tracy seized the newspaper and flipped the pages over.

There would probably be a formal death notice as well as the obituary. Yes, there it was, very short and businesslike, with no mention of the family. Tracy read it swiftly, noting the time and place of the funeral, then sat back to wrestle with the biggest temptation she had ever experienced.

It was at a London church she had never heard of, which meant that there might be quite a good-sized congregation, since presumably David Lincoln's former colleagues would turn up. She could easily mingle with them and remain unnoticed, and she would be able to see Andrew again.

She spent ten minutes making plans, deciding what she would tell her mother—no problem since a day in London was easily accounted for— and what time she would need to start in order not to be late. Luckily there was a fast train service from the outer suburb where they lived.

It was all arranged in her head, all neat and tidy and feasible, when the utter idiocy of it struck her like a physical blow. She must be out of her mind! What would be the point of it all? Where was the sense in pandering to dreams? Much better to forget as quickly as possible, and the way to do that was to get down to some really hard work.

The agency rang up on the morning of the funeral.

'I've got a job which is right up your street, dear,' said the owner. 'Can you get away today, because it's urgent?'

'Where is it?' Tracy asked eagerly.

'Sevenoaks. I believe you're quite near the M25, aren't you? You should be able to drive there in less than an hour.'

'Yes, I could. What sort of case is it?'

'A very severe stroke. Mrs Campbell is eighty-four and the family don't want her to go into hospital. It could easily be a terminal case, but I know you'll be able to cope.'

'I hope so.' Tracy scribbled down the address. 'I'll get off as soon as I've packed a suitcase.'

She had no qualms about leaving her mother at this stage, and as she hurried upstairs to pack she thought thankfully that it was a very good thing she hadn't given in to that crazy notion of going to London. Much better to be dashing off in the opposite direction to tackle what was bound to be an arduous job.

In Gibraltar she had worn a white uniform dress at the hospital, but when working in England she preferred the discreet dark blue of a sister. Three dresses were hanging in her wardrobe all ready, and she packed them hastily, together with a few clothes for her off-duty time. From what she had been told about the case, it didn't look as though there would be much of that!

She was carrying everything downstairs when the phone rang again. Impatiently she snatched the receiver and rattled off the number.

There was a slight pause, then a voice said, 'Can I speak to Tracy, please?'

She heard herself give a faint gasp, but no words would come, and the voice said anxiously, 'Have I got the wrong number? I want to speak to Tracy Arnold.'

She made a huge effort to stop behaving like a moron and answer him. 'It's all right, Andrew. You haven't got the wrong number, and this is Tracy speaking.'

'It doesn't sound anything like you.'

'I was surprised, that's all,' she explained hastily.

'I'm over here for my uncle's funeral——'

'I saw his death in the paper. I'm so sorry, Andrew—I know how you felt about him.'

'I must admit I do feel rather bereft,' Andrew admitted. 'He was all the family I had.'

Tracy wanted to fling her arms round him and tell him he wasn't alone, he still had her, and all her love as well.

But instead of that she merely repeated that she was sorry, adding, 'I'm just off to start a job and it's an urgent one, so —— '

'So you'd like me to stop delaying you?' Before she could think of a way of answering which wouldn't be hurtful, he continued speaking.

'Actually, I was ringing up to see if you could have dinner with me this evening, but I see now that it's quite impossible.'

'I would have loved it, Andrew.' For the first time in the stilted conversation her voice was full of sincerity. 'But, as you've already said, it's out of the question.'

'Perhaps another time,' he said vaguely. 'I have to fly back tomorrow, but I shall be coming over again to deal with various matters. Goodbye for now, Tracy. It's been great to have had this brief conversation.'

She murmured something and replaced the receiver. For a moment she stood by the telephone deep in thought. Had Andrew rung up because he was sad and lonely, or did he *really* want to see her? On the whole she was inclined to think it was the former—or was that because she didn't dare to believe anything else?

The job at Sevenoaks turned out to be every bit as tough as Tracy had desired, in spite of the luxury of her surroundings. Mrs Campbell was a wealthy woman who had led an independent life in quite a large house, looked after by a resident married couple. As the agency had warned, the stroke was a very severe one, and Tracy found herself having to cope with a totally helpless patient whose misshapen features gave no clue to her thoughts—if she had any, which seemed very doubtful.

The female half of the married couple was fortunately willing to help with lifting, and a woman living nearby, who had had some nursing experience, took charge at night, provided Tracy was prepared to consider herself on call. The system worked very well, but it meant she was either on duty or on call for the whole of the twenty-four hours, and sometimes she felt guilty because she knew the agency would not have approved.

As for her own personal feelings, she didn't mind at all. Free time was something she had no use for at present.

But after she had been there five days, the situation changed.

To begin with, she noticed a slight improvement in her patient, and the doctor confirmed it. He was a nice, friendly man and he congratulated Tracy on her nursing.

'You're looking rather tired.' He eyed her keenly and clearly disapproved of shadowed eyes and pale cheeks. 'Have you been taking your proper free time?'

'Well, not exactly, but——'

'I thought as much.' He glanced at the window where raindrops were chasing each other downwards. 'As soon as the weather improves you're to go for a good walk. Mrs Campbell will be all right with her housekeeper for a couple of hours.' And, with his hand on the doorknob, he added severely, 'That's an order.'

Tracy liked him and did not want to arouse his displeasure by disobedience. Consequently she was glad when it continued to rain, but towards evening the sky lightened and the sun came out. The forecast for the next day was good, and she made up her mind to do as she had been told and take the afternoon off.

When Andrew's telephone call came it seemed like a miracle that she had it all so neatly arranged.

'You're wanted on the phone, Nurse,' the housekeeper told her, eyeing her with a flicker of interest. 'A gentleman with a nice voice. Your boyfriend, maybe?'

'I haven't got one.'

Hurrying downstairs, Tracy found her pulses reacting strangely, yet she felt sure it couldn't be Andrew, because he didn't know where she was.

'Tracy Arnold speaking,' she said briskly.

'You sound very businesslike! Is it because you're on a case?'

'Andrew!' Her heart leapt in her breast and she nearly choked. 'How on earth—I mean, I don't see how you could know where to find me——'

'Your mother knew where you were and it was she who gave me the number. She said she was sure you wouldn't mind.'

'Of course I don't mind.' Tracy hesitated, then added bravely, 'I'm very pleased.'

'That makes two of us.' His voice, which had been casually friendly, suddenly deepened. 'Listen, love, I want to see you—I want it very badly. Is there any chance?'

She wanted it too—quite desperately.

'But where are you?' she asked. 'Gibraltar? London?'

'Neither. Afraid I've got rather a shock for you. I'm in Sevenoaks. I've been seeing my uncle's solicitors in town, and when they'd finished with me I hired a car and drove down in the hope of seeing you.' His tone became urgent. 'You haven't said yet whether it's possible——'

'I'm free this afternoon and I'd planned to go for a good walk,' she told him. 'I promised the doctor——'

'You're under a doctor?' Andrew interrupted anxiously.

'No, no—I meant my patient's doctor. He thinks I've been sticking too close to the job and he ordered me some exercise in the fresh air.' She hesitated, then added lightly, 'You can come with me if you like.'

'Exactly what I had in mind. Have you ever been in the park at Knole?'

'Only when I was taken round the house as a child. I don't remember much about it. I expect I was a bit young to appreciate stately homes.'

'I wasn't proposing we should visit the house— that would hardly be what the doctor ordered.'

They arranged to meet in a car park, and hung up. In a fever of impatience Tracy began to count the hours and then the minutes. At the last moment she tore off the green patterned dress she had chosen with so much care and substituted a blue one which, she had suddenly remembered, Andrew had once said he liked.

Not that it mattered what she wore. He had given no hint that he intended anything more than a friendly meeting.

Nevertheless her hands were shaking so much when she parked her car in Sevenoaks that she had to make three attempts at getting it straight. Hoping Andrew hadn't been watching, she got out and looked round nervously. At first she could see no sign of him and then, suddenly, he was there—coming towards her with long strides.

'Oh, Tracy!' He took both her hands in his and held them tightly. 'It's been such a long time!'

'Almost a month.'

'It feels like three months.' Slipping his arm into hers, he went on, 'We'll have to start our walk here, because you can't take cars into the park at Knole unless you're going to visit the house. It's not far.'

'I don't mind.'

She had answered at random, and the small part of her brain which was continuing to function normally dealt similarly with the disjointed remarks they exchanged during the walk through streets. When they came to the gates, Andrew released her arm and took her hand instead, quickening his step slightly as they followed a broad well-kept path.

Tracy kept pace with him in a daze of bitter-sweet emotion. What all this was leading to she couldn't possibly guess—perhaps nothing except a sentimental reunion—but just for the moment for her to be with Andrew again was enough.

They left the path, turning their backs on the great house, and began to walk on grass. There were more trees now, casting great pools of shade on the springy turf, and gradually they left the everyday world behind them and entered a cool green area where there was only dappled sunshine and the trees grew close together, their leaves scarcely stirring. A wonderful, secret world where they were the only inhabitants.

'Have you had enough exercise?' Andrew asked.

'For the time being.'

'Let's sit down, then. This grassy bank looks comfortable.'

Every nerve stretched like violin strings, Tracy propped herself on her elbows and wondered if he could hear the thudding of her heart. Sitting bolt upright beside her, he looked no more relaxed than she felt.

There was no sound except the intermittent singing of birds and the drone of a plane. A rabbit came out of its burrow and began to nibble the grass, and a grey squirrel raced down a tree-trunk, glanced at them indifferently and vanished round the other side.

'We've got a lot to talk about,' Andrew said suddenly.

'Have we?'

'I have anyway, but first I want to ask you a

question.' He turned his head and looked down at her. 'Do you remember that evening when you came to dinner at the flat?'

'Of course.'

'I wanted to make love to you so much, Tracy, but——' He seemed unable to finish the sentence and asked instead, 'Would you have let me?'

For a moment Tracy was transported back to the quiet, lamplit room and the intoxicating nearness of his body stretched out beside her on the sofa. She had longed for fulfilment then, and at the same time had been grateful to him for his control.

'I don't think it's fair to ask me that,' she protested.

'Probably not, but I'd very much like a reply.'

Tracy did her best to give an honest answer. 'I might, but I'm sure I would have regretted it afterwards. I've never gone in for casual love-making, and the only time I let it happen I was left feeling disturbed and angry with myself. It's probably very silly of me, but that's the way I am.'

The reply seemed to satisfy him. He lay back and rolled on to his side, very close to her arm. His fingers began to fondle the bare flesh, sending sensuous tremors of delight over her whole body.

'That night at the flat—it wouldn't have been casual for me,' he said quietly.

Bewildered, her pulses racing, Tracy glanced at him, but found herself unable to meet his steady blue gaze. She wanted so desperately to believe he meant what he appeared to be saying—and was afraid to.

'I'm sorry,' she said helplessly, 'I don't understand.'

'I wanted something much deeper than a one-off occasion, but I didn't think you were feeling like that at all.' His voice deepened with emotion. 'I love you, Tracy darling, and I want to make love to you most desperately right now this minute.'

'You love me?' she repeated in a wondering tone, and for a moment there was such a song of joy inside her she felt her heart would burst.

'That's what I said, and that's what I meant.' He gave her a tender smile. 'I even love you when you're being argumentative—and I can't say fairer than that!'

Tracy's own emotions were threatening to swamp her, but somehow she clung to sanity. This was no time for pretence. She had to be truthful or regret it forever.

'I love you too, Andrew. I have for a long time. And I want you to make love to me—I want it with every bit of me, body and mind and heart, but not here—not in a public park——'

'Oh, how I wish we were back at the flat!' He put his hands on her shoulders, his eyes raking her face. 'Did you really say you loved me? I didn't dream it?'

'I really said it, and I meant it, but——' Suddenly she was overwhelmed with tears and put both hands over her face to hide them.

'Darling, what's the matter?' Andrew tried to pull her hands away, but she resisted him.

'I—I don't think an affair would be a good idea with you in Gibraltar—or even London—and me working all over the place. We'd make each other miserable—it just wouldn't work out right for us——'

He leapt to his feet with so much vigour that the rabbit fled, 'Who said anything about an affair? I want to *marry* you, you lunatic—yes, even though you've got all sorts of hang-ups about marriage. I don't *care*, do you hear? I intend my marriage to be a success, and if you're going to be the other half of it you'll have to go along with that too.'

Tracy gazed at him incredulously, and suddenly her eyes were like stars and there was a song of joy in her heart, but still she hardly dared to believe him. He had such high ideals where marriage was concerned, and her own outlook had hitherto been so completely different.

Andrew had paused for a reply, waiting anxiously yet hopefully, but, finding her tongue-tied, he dropped to his knees and leaned forward with a hand on either side of her.

'Please tell me you'll be the other half, Tracy love—don't keep me in suspense!'

'Oh, Andrew, I can't imagine anything more wonderful but——'

'But you're still scared of committing yourself to that sort of relationship?' His voice was anguished and the pain in his eyes wrenched at her emotions.

'I didn't mean that—at least, not exactly—but I've believed for such a long time that marriage was too big a risk, and I didn't want to fall in love—really, properly in love—for quite a while, perhaps never, *because* of the risk, and so——' She broke off, conscious of a hopelessly tangled sentence.

'And so you've still got qualms,' he said bitterly.

'I didn't say that! At least, I didn't mean to. I was just trying to explain how I *used* to feel, but I got so mixed up I didn't get around to telling you that—that I've changed——'

'Changed? You mean you *don't* feel like that any more? Oh, Tracy——'

'I had a lot of time for thinking when I was looking after my mother and I realised how stupid and—and cowardly I'd been to let myself be so influenced by other people.' Tracy took a deep breath. 'The only risk that bothered me then was the risk of losing you—in fact, it was more than a risk. I really thought I'd thrown away something which might have turned into a chance of real happiness.' She stopped with a tremulous smile. 'Oh, dear, I'm getting incoherent again!'

The pain in his eyes which had so grieved her had turned into rapture. With a stifled sound that was almost a groan he took her in his arms, and her whole body responded ecstatically to the depth of their shared emotion. His kiss was long and passionate, and she wished it would go on for ever. Lying back on the soft sweet-smelling grass, she felt as though she were floating on a tide of happiness.

After a while Andrew stirred.

'Put it into words, Tracy darling—tell me you'll marry me. I want you for always—to be mine and bear my children——and together we'll make a happy home for us all. Will you do that—please?'

'I will,' she promised, and it seemed to her that the vow she had just made in that quiet, secret place was every bit as solemn and binding as the one she would make later in church.

AN EXCITING NEW SERIAL BY ONE OF THE WORLD'S BESTSELLING WRITERS OF ROMANCE

BARBARY WHARF is an exciting 6 book mini-series set in the glamorous world of international journalism.

Powerful media tycoon Nick Caspian wants to take control of the Sentinel, an old and well established British newspaper group, but opposing him is equally determined Gina Tyrell, whose loyalty to the Sentinel and all it stands for is absolute.

The drama, passion and heartache that passes between Nick and Gina continues throughout the series - and in addition to this, each novel features a separate romance for you to enjoy.

Read all about Hazel and Piet's dramatic love affair in the first part of this exciting new serial.

BESIEGED

Available soon

Price: £2.99

Available from Boots, Martins, John Menzies, W.H. Smith, most supermarkets and other paperback stockists.
Also available from Mills & Boon Reader Service, PO Box 236, Thornton Road, Croydon, Surrey CR9 3RU.

ESCAPE TO THE RUGGED OUTBACK, EXPERIENCE THE GLAMOUR OF SYDNEY, AND RELAX ON A PARADISE ISLAND...

Four new Romances set in Australia for you to enjoy.

WILD TEMPTATION – Elizabeth Duke
WOMAN AT WILLAGONG CREEK – Jessica Hart
ASKING FOR TROUBLE – Miranda Lee
ISLAND OF DREAMS – Valerie Parv

Look out for these scintillating love stories from April 1992

Price: £6.40

*Available from Boots, Martins, John Menzies, W.H. Smith, most supermarkets and other paperback stockists.
Also available from Mills & Boon Reader Service, PO Box 236, Thornton Road, Croydon, Surrey CR9 3RU.*

—MEDICAL ROMANCE—

The books for enjoyment this month are:

DEMPSEY'S DILEMMA Christine Adams
WIND OF CHANGE Clare Lavenham
DOCTOR ON SKYE Margaret O'Neill
CROSSROADS OF THE HEART Judith Worthy

♥ ♥ ♥ ♥ ♥

Treats in store!

Watch next month for the following absorbing stories:

SAVING DR GREGORY Caroline Anderson
FOR LOVE'S SAKE ONLY Margaret Barker
THE WRONG DIAGNOSIS Drusilla Douglas
ENCOUNTER WITH A SURGEON Janet Ferguson

Available from Boots, Martins, John Menzies, W.H. Smith, most supermarkets and other paperback stockists.

Also available from Mills & Boon Reader Service, P.O. Box 236, Thornton Road, Croydon, Surrey CR9 3RU.

Readers in South Africa - write to:
Book Services International Ltd, P.O. Box 41654, Craighall, Transvaal 2024.